Before the Wind

Before the Wind

LLOYD M. MOXON

Doubleday & Company, Inc.
Garden City, New York
1978

TO:

Poseidon and All of His Sons.

Library of Congress Cataloging in Publication Data

Library of Congress Catalog Card Number 77-27715

HOISTING THE SAILS

from Beaumont and Fletcher

Lay her before the wind, up with your canvas,
And let her work, the wind begins to whistle;
Clap all her streamers on, and let her dance
As if she were the minion of the ocean.
Let her bestride the billows, till they roar,
And curl their wanton heads.
The day grows fair and clear, and the wind
*   courts us.*
O! for a lusty sail now, to give chase to,
A stubborn bark, that would but bear up to us,
And 'change a broadside bravely!

This verse was printed in the 1802 *Navy Chronicle,* the semi-official journal of the British Navy.

Chapter 1

The wind had freshened and was whipping up the waters of the Thames into waves as it blew spume and spray into the yellow varnished wherry. The boatman was sculling me to the fleet anchorage at Spithead, but the current and the waves were slowing our passage. I sat midships in the water boat and clutched my boat cloak tightly around my new lieutenant's uniform wishing for a tarpaulin as I felt the moisture penetrate beneath the cloak. Damn, if I hadn't tried to pinch pennies, I could have taken a wherry with two men at oars. If I had done so, I would have arrived at my new ship in a more immaculate state. Joining my first ship as lieutenant, I did want to look presentable.

I shouldn't complain, at least I had a ship. February of 1795 marked two years of war with the French Revolutionaries, but ships were still less available than lieutenants. If I hadn't served with Pellew, I doubt that I would have had this assignment. Lucky Pellew had fought the first frigate battle of the war and won. As a result, he became Sir Edward and not too much later was given a more powerful frigate. I had served under him as a midshipman when he was plain Captain Pellew and followed him from the *Nymphe* to the *Arethusa*. Yes, Pellew was favored by fortune and some of that favor rubbed off onto others. In that first battle between the *Cléopâtre* and the *Nymphe,* I had been lucky too; I survived. Two of my fellow midshipmen and two of our lieutenants were wounded; twenty-three seamen died. Pellew was knighted and his brother, Commander Israel Pellew, who was a supernumerary on our ship, was made post captain. I remained a midshipman. More recently, some of that Pellew luck had come my way. When I took my examination for lieutenant, the board, finding that I had served under Sir Edward on both the *Nymphe* and the *Arethusa,* were most kind with their questions. The greatest part of the examination was spent in my recounting the battle with the *Cléopâtre.* As the senior captain said when congratulating me on passing, "You'll do well, St. John, after all, you're one of Pellew's lads, you know."

A change in the motion of the wherry disturbed my thoughts; the wherryman was starting to back water to allow a large snow the right of way. After the two-master passed, he resumed his sculling. I was to join the *Monmouth,* 64. It would seem strange to serve in a two-decker after almost two years in frigates. I was disappointed in the assignment, for there is much to say in favor of service in frigates, not the least being a better chance at prize money. I had just been commissioned lieutenant; no frigate captain was searching for a replacement. Any service afloat was better than being stranded on the beach at half pay. I was glad to get the assignment to the liner, for the only income I had was my service pay. If I had been discharged yesterday, before I was commissioned, I would have had no money at all, for beached midshipmen do not receive even half pay.

We were close to the line of anchored ships now. "Zur," said the boatman, "that be the *Monmouth.*"

I looked at the ship he indicated. From the water's surface, the ship was most impressive; it seemed to tower up above the water like a lusty, young mountain, but it was only a sixty-four-gun ship. The larger 74's ruled the wave, making service on a 64 hazardous. Given a choice, I would have avoided such service, but the Admiralty dictates and newly commissioned officers have no option but to say, "Aye aye," and follow orders.

From the bow of the two-decker, a lookout shouted, "Boat, ahoy!"

The wherryman spat his cud of tobacco out into the water and then cupped his palms into a speaking trumpet; he shouted, "Aye aye," so loudly my ears rang. It was the customary and hoary old practice of telling those aboard ship that one of the ship's officers was approaching. We were close to the liner now; I could see the large gallery, double-decked, projecting out behind the stern windows. The *Monmouth* was an old ship; it had numerous, intricate carvings decorating the stern transom. Many captains would have gilded these carvings, or at least picked out the work with yellow paint. The scrollwork and figures were innocent of paint or gilt except for a faded few patches. Whoever her captain was, he didn't believe in show.

We were at the chains now, but instead of hooking on, the wherryman held his boat with his scull. I handed him the agreed-on fare, and then as the waves lifted the small boat, I sprang for the chains and started to scuttle up. Someone aboard dropped a whip down for the boatman to attach my chest and then lifted it up past me and onto the deck. I continued to climb. As I stepped through the entry port out onto the deck, I removed my hat and said, "Come aboard," to the lieutenant who greeted me. I started to put my hat back on, but he shook his head, frowned and pointed. My eyes followed the direction of his forefinger. The entire crew of the *Monmouth* were mustered on deck and were standing in formation with their hats off. It was a Tuesday, but the chaplain was conducting a religious service. As I watched, the minister started to wave his arms and a cacophonous dirge arose from the assembled men. They were singing a hymn; loud it was, but far from melodious. I have always enjoyed fine music. When I lived in London, I attended concerts regularly. I never missed a single German or Italian maestro. Fine music uplifts the soul, but when you get a herd of British seamen bellowing out a hymn, it sounds like a drove of cattle at the slaughterhouse. The song ended as suddenly as it began. A petty officer shouted, "Dismissed!" The seamen replaced their caps and broke formation. Some of them disappeared below, while others started their chores on the deck. The head pumps were rigged and the decks wet down so the men could start holystoning them.

I looked at the lieutenant; he was a long, spare-looking individual, spare to the point of emaciation. His most prominent feature was an immense Adam's-apple that bobbed wildly up and down when he started to speak to me. He had heavy, well-arched eyebrows and a habit of raising the left one intermittently. This supercilious gesture made him look foolish. He was a tall man, almost as tall as my six feet one, but he must have weighed three stone less than I. "John Sinjin," I said.

"I'm Pierce Hallowell," he answered. "What date's your commission, St. John?"

"Yesterday, February 18, 1795."

A beatific smile lit his face. "My commission is dated September 9, 1794." He had reason enough to smile. For so long as we both were lieutenants, he would be senior to me. "I'm the third lieutenant; you will be fourth."

Looking away from Hallowell, I glanced around the deck of the ship. It was an impressive sight, a fearsome fighting machine armed with 18- and 24-pounders, twenty-six of each plus a dozen 9's. Not counted in rating the number of guns were eight 32-pounder carronades and numerous swivels and howitzers. Yes, the battery carried by the *Monmouth* was impressive, even more impressive when compared to the field guns used by the Army. Six-pounder field guns are but puny slings when compared to the heavy guns on the liner. The Army does use some heavy guns for siege purposes, but a complete land siege train would have fewer cannon than one two-decker. A siege train, if the fields are not muddy, can move a few miles each day; the *Monmouth* could carry her vast batteries two hundred miles in twenty-four hours if the winds were favorable.

As impressive and formidable as the *Monmouth* appeared, it was passé, having been outclassed by the newer, stronger 74's. Some of the sixty-four-gun ships were being called in to convert to frigates. As I stood there, I was overcome with the realization that unless this ship were relegated, converted, or I received an independent command, I would be stuck here for years. It might well be my home until the war with France ended.

"I'll have your dunnage sent below," said Hallowell, looking around for a warm body to carry my chest. "You there, Simms, take Lieutenant St. John's sea chest below."

The seaman said, "Aye aye, sir," wiped his hands on his striped jersey, and came aft to pick up my chest. As he bent over, he broke wind loudly, but did not hesitate or apologize. He grabbed the chest and hoisted it to his shoulder. I could see his muscles rippling. "Folley me, sir," he said, and started down a hatchway.

I did not remain to bid fairwell to Hallowell, instead I followed the man. He deposited my chest in a small cubicle no more than six feet on a side. This was to be my home. Despite the fact that the *Monmouth* was the bigger ship, the cubicle seemed no larger than the space occupied by the fourth lieutenant of my last ship, the *Arethusa*. The built-in cot had been designed for a man of average height, but I had long ago learned how to sleep in a fetal position. The deck beams were a good five feet eight inches above the deck. I would still have to duck when I entered my cabin, but I wouldn't have to crouch and squat-walk. For the average-sized man, there would be ample headroom. As I looked around the little room, I could see why it had been assigned to the lowliest of the lieutenants aboard the liner. The squat, ugly breech of a 24-pounder gun intruded into the cabin, robbing it of living space. "Oh well, Sinjin, me boy," I said to myself, "you'll jist have t' make do, now, won'tcha. It's a damn sight better than living in the cockpit with the midshipmen."

After hanging up my boat cloak and putting on a pea jacket—it was damned cold that February—I went back topside. I had to pay my respects to the captain. It wouldn't do to wind up in his black book for lack of naval etiquette. Work parties were busy up on the deck, swabbing, mopping, and holystoning the decks to a pristine white. Each group of working seamen was supervised by a petty officer who stood over them, rope starter in hand, to make sure they did not slack off and neglect their job. The stone prayer books made a rasping sound against the oak of the decks.

The yards of the two-decker were crossed and she looked ready for sea. I wondered how long we would remain here at Spithead, but speculation answers no questions. I abandoned the thought and made my way up the companionway to the quarterdeck. Hallowell, that gawky loon of a man, was the only officer on the poop. In the absence of the captain, he was pacing up and down on the sanctified weather side of the quarterdeck. If the captain were to appear suddenly, he would scuttle over to the lee side, but in the absence of higher authority, he had the option of using that area. I joined him and we paced together, hands clasped firmly behind our backs, a habit learned by all officers when midshipmen to prevent that heinous crime of placing hands in pockets. As we reached the end of the deck, we turned inward toward each other thus allowing us to converse without presenting our backsides to one another. "I say, Hallowell, I must report to the captain."

He did not answer, but drew an enormous silver watch from his fob pocket. "It's 'bout ten minutes to five bells. The cap'n requested that you report to him then."

"Aye," I said, "since we have a few minutes to converse, tell me about the *Monmouth*. Is it a happy ship?"

He extended his index finger, pointing it toward the skylight projecting through the quarterdeck, then placed that finger across his lips while he raised his eyebrow in that ridiculous, supercilious manner. I understood immediately that someone in the captain's day cabin might be listening. "Yes, St. John," he said, "it's a most happy ship for it's a Christian ship. The Lord is with us for we ask His guidance and blessing every morning."

That explained the prayer meeting on Tuesday. Church services every day; the captain must be mad, mad as the proverbial loon. I thought that I had troubles when I served aboard the *Nymphe* and the *Arethusa*. Sir Edward was so impetuous; he would rather fight than play whist, and he was most partial to a social game of cards. His rushing to battle had frightened me until I realized that even in a close fight very few men are killed. I was almost in a panic whenever we were engaged before I learned this. Fewer men were lost in battle than were taken by disease or accidents. Rum kills more sailors than bullets. After making this discovery, I was able to appear as brave as the rest of them. They thought me a gallant soul, but inwardly I was still a coward. Here on the *Monmouth* I had a praying fool instead of a fighting fool to lead me. It would undoubtedly be safer, but the thought of church services daily dismayed me.

I'm not an atheist, decidedly not; I'm a good Church of England man. Before joining the service, I went to church religiously, at least once a month. Pellew conducted a weekly service which I had attended since joining the Navy. That was a little frequent for my taste, but at sea I had nowhere else to go. What bothered me most about the daily church services aboard the *Monmouth* was the strong dissenter flavor to the partial service I had heard.

It was time to report to the captain. I walked down the ladder to his cabin. A burly, bloody bullock, a marine in a red uniform with pipe-clayed belts, was standing guard at the door. He presented his bayoneted musket and I knocked. "Enter," called the captain. I did and stood at attention, my cocked hat under my left elbow. I had my best uniform on, the new one, and my shoes with the gold buckles. The captain, seated behind an ornate table, looked back at me. He was an old man, I thought at first, but then realized that his appearance belied his age. He had a great trumpet of a nose, one of those immense sculptures usually found only on the very old. That noble edifice combined with an ascetic, starved look made him appear old beyond his years; he must have been in his late fifties, but he looked as if he were at least five and sixty. His skin was an almost translucent parchment, the bleached color of virgin foolscap. His pale blue eyes looked weak and watery until he began to speak; then they blazed with a fanatic glow that I had only seen in lunatics and dedicated vegetarians. "Welcome aboard, Mr. St. John. We run a Christian ship. All officers have volunteered to eschew their liquor ration; I

expect you to do likewise." He smiled at me when he said
that and began industriously to mine his nose.

What a captain expects is an order. On board a king's
ship, the captain ranks higher than God. "Of course, sir," I
said out loud, but thought to myself, that's a pile of hen
dung, you sanctimonious old bastard.

"We shall expect to see you at prayer service each morning. When the ship is anchored, all hands attend the service except for lookouts and the officer of the deck." He
paused to hide the results of his mining expedition on the
underside of his table, then continued. "When we're at
sea, the off-duty watch attends the first service. At eight
bells, they relieve the others and we hold the second service. Now, St. John, I have some literature for you to read.
You will familiarize yourself with this." Captain Gamble
handed me a sheaf of poor quality paper covered with
small print. "Dismissed, Lieutenant. You will have the
next watch, so you had better make ready." He pulled a
large handkerchief from his sleeve and blew his nose; it
even sounded like a trumpet—loud, harsh, and resonant.

"Aye aye, sir," I replied and left his cabin. As I walked
away, I glanced at the literature. "Methodist claptrap," I
grumbled. "Captain Gamble, Captain William bloody
Gamble!" It was no wonder that he was known throughout
the service as "Holy Bill." I still had the tracts in my hand;
I folded them and shoved the papers into the pocket of my
peacoat. Lord, what does a junior officer have to put up
with? I thought. Here I was, a good Church of England
man, and the captain turns out to be some kind of dissent-
ing Methodist missionary.

Back in my cubbyhole, I first checked my sextant case.
The sextant seemed in good shape. I lifted the tray and
pulled out my own Arnold chronometer. Many captains
did not own one, but my uncle had given it to me when

first I joined the Navy. I had wound the instrument that morning, but I hadn't checked my watch against it. The watch was a good one, but it could lose up to three minutes a day. By resetting it just before noon every day, I could use the watch instead of the chronometer when we checked for longitude. When and if I ever was master of my own ship, I could openly display the Arnold, but until that day it would be a shade ostentatious to use it before less fortunate individuals. I snapped the rear cover open and glanced at the inscription on the inside for perhaps the six hundredth time.

> To my nephew, John St. John, in
> anticipation of that day he is
> posted captain.
> 13 January 1793
> Vice Admiral John Bacon, K.B.

I put the chronometer back in the case and then removed my good uniform, carefully putting it into a japanned tin box. I would be on duty soon and my old midshipman's uniform was good enough. The sailmaker on the *Arethusa* had cut the white tabs off the collar and cuffs to convert it to proper wear for a lieutenant. A pair of neatly darned white stockings and old shoes with pinchbeck buckles were fitting additions to the old, sea-faded uniform. I had an hour before my watch went on duty, so I curled up on my cot and tried to relax.

The ship's bell tolled; eight times the clarion note sounded; it was noon. The forenoon watch was ending; my watch, the afternoon watch, was beginning. I dashed up the ladders to the quarterdeck to find the captain conversing with two other officers. These must be the first and second lieutenants, I thought as I looked at them. The older of the two, was a very foppish-looking individual, a real gentleman type, rather lah-di-dah, with lace cuffs and the most elegant lieutenant's uniform I had ever seen. I caught a whiff of an expensive French perfume and presumed it was coming from him, for neither the captain nor the other officer seemed the type to employ scent. He was a handsome man with smooth, even features, but he no more looked alive than a Gainsborough painting. This naval version of the "Blue Boy" had a small, mud-colored dog with inordinately long ears snuffling at his heels; it was a cocking spaniel. I've always favored spaniels, especially the larger springer, but the dog looked as vacuous as its owner. I wondered if on this God-fearing ship we had a hunter, but could remember no passage in the Bible that forbade hunting. Even the commandment, "Thou shalt not kill," seemed flexible if you told yourself that God was on our side. After all, the French were a race of breast thumpers, papists.

"Man the capstan!" shouted the captain. We were getting under way.

Since the senior officers had no time to pay attention to me, I studied the other man. God, but he was big, no, he was huge. The man was a full two boarding axes across his shoulders and even more across his butt. With all his girth, he stood only five feet six or so. I glanced at his middle; it was a proper Falstaffian belly, straining against his breeches as if it were well lined with capon. In contrast to the first lieutenant, the fop, this man was an utter slob, dressed in a faded, patched uniform.

The deck of the liner bustled with activity as a horde of seamen poured up on deck to fit the bars into the square slots of the capstan head. With a two-decker, the capstan would have a double head. On a lower deck, other seamen were fitting bars to the other head. The capstan bars were long, twenty-eight feet long; ten or more men to each bar were required. The seamen put their shoulders to the spokes and started to walk the immense anchor off the bottom of the river. To ease their labors, a fiddler scratched out a tune. Like a blind mule grinding corn, the men walked in a circle. Their efforts snaked the anchor cable through the hawsepipes so that the ship's boys could nip the cable to the follower and guide it to the cable tier. I was just a supernumerary here on the quarterdeck; as a new officer, I wouldn't be trusted with the delicate task of getting under way. I was only a spectator; I relaxed and enjoyed the entertainment. The rigging of the ship swarmed with topmen scrambling up the shrouds to handle the sails. The braces, those heavy ropes which attach to the yards, were picked up and held by lines of waisters. They were ready to haul the yards on command. The yards could be turned to let the sails catch the wind.

"Hove short!" cried a voice from the fo'c'sle.

"Mainsail haul!" shouted the captain, so loudly that his alabaster skin turned plum red. The sails were sheeted home; the anchor hauled in and catted in place on the outside of the bow; the ship, under way, headed down river.

On the other ships still at anchor, the crews had turned out to see us depart. I could see the glint of many telescopes both on the anchored ships and on shore. Our evolutions had been watched and rated by experts; I wondered how well we had performed. From my point of view, I had to concede a workmanlike job to Captain Gamble. "Holy Bill" was a good seaman, but he lacked the panache, the flair, of a Pellew. I also wondered where we were going. We had so many options; the flag of Britain flew all over the world and her ships were to be found wheresoever there might be enough water to float a rowboat. We might be heading for Gibraltar or Malta, to India, Canada, the West Indies, or even the South Seas. The captain hadn't chosen to confide his instructions to me; he might not have opened them yet. Eventually, all aboard the ship would know our destination. The only difference it could make, wherever it might be, would be the climate. All of us aboard this ship would work, eat, and pray daily; hoping for the sight of an enemy vessel and a chance for prize money.

Chapter 2

A ship is a community. The peasants and common folk live
before the mast, the gentry aft. Like any village, gossip flies
on the wings of rumor. It wasn't long before the entire
crew of the *Monmouth* knew the ship's destination. The
captain's clerk, wishing to show off his superiority, had
dropped a word into an attentive ear. The word was passed
around the scuttlebutts, with the rum ration and with the
mess kids. I had thought of many exotic places we might
have been sent, but realization was much less than expecta-
tion. The ship was headed for Brest. We were joining the
channel fleet to blockade France.

The crew of the *Monmouth*, for the most part, were experienced; they had served with the channel fleet before. I
was beginning to single out individuals among the men. By
the time we finished this cruise, I expected to know each of
the five hundred twenty-six men aboard. Already, some of
the stronger personalities were felt. Unfortunately, a man
chooses his friends, God chooses his relatives, and the Admiralty chooses his shipmates. If I had any part in the selec-
tion, I would have made numerous other choices starting
with Captain William Gamble and First Lieutenant Melvin Lloyd. There were a group of seamen aboard the *Monmouth* that I mentally classified as the "deacons." These

whoresons were the captain's toadies, every man of them. Together they formed a formidable spy system, keeping Gamble informed of every infraction of his rules, especially those regarding religious observance. The chief among these blots was the master-at-arms, Mr. Skuggs. Short, scrawny, and ferret-faced, Skuggs had been born within the sound of Bow bells; this fact was attested to by his cockney accent. More than once I found him furtively spying on me.

The officers were an easier matter to know, for there were fewer of them. Our esteemed first lieutenant, Melvin Lloyd by name, was an incompetent. He would stride around the ship followed by his cocking spaniel and acting as if he knew what to do, but in over twenty years of service, he had been unable to persuade the Admiralty to advance him to post rank despite excellent political connections. The only reason I could see for his presence aboard the *Monmouth* was nepotism; Lloyd was the captain's first cousin. The second lieutenant was a contrast to the exquisite Lloyd. Big, burly, and slovenly he was, but he was a fine seaman. John Gamble was the captain's nephew, but there was no nepotism involved here. He hated the ship, hated his uncle, and was the only man aboard that managed to avoid the church services. He had also refused to take the non-drinking pledge and was the sole officer to receive his rum ration. If his uncle hadn't needed him, he would have been transferred off the ship, which would have pleased him but left the captain in a bind, for John Gamble was the only experienced, competent officer aboard other than the captain himself. Young Hallowell, like me, was a newly made lieutenant. He seemed to have the makings of a fine officer, but he needed maturing, as I did.

Most of the midshipmen aboard were a nondescript lot

of sniveling, whining lads. All but one of them were new aboard the ship. The exception was another Gamble, Mr. Beverley Gamble Perkins, another nephew. Young Perkins at eighteen was considerably older than the other midshipmen. I learned later that he had just failed his lieutenant's examination after being appointed acting lieutenant. His failure was the reason I was aboard. His uncle would have preferred young Perkins to be fourth lieutenant, but until he could find an amenable board of captains and have the midshipman promoted he needed another lieutenant.

There was a certain fulsome quality about Perkins, a grossness of spirit and body that produced an instant dislike, almost an antipathy. The feeling seemed mutual. Perkins looked like what would have been produced if the princess kissed a frog and got a human frog instead of a prince. A huge, sloping head grew from his shoulders without benefit of neck. His eyes bulged and his complexion was a sort of yellow green, more charitably described as sallow. Where a frog had freckles, Perkins had deep smallpox pits, making his face look as if the devil had stamped over it while wearing his hobnailed boots. He even had the habit of flicking his tongue between his lips and quickly withdrawing it. This mannerism made him look as if he were trying to catch flies. I disliked the man on sight and he hated me for taking the position he thought rightfully his.

I had been on deck during the first dog watch. When relieved, I hurried to my cabin for an hour's relaxation before the call for the first church service. As I came down the ladder, I saw what looked like a midshipman leave my cubicle and dash off. It had to be young Perkins; all the other midshipmen were shorter and leaner than he. I dashed for my cabin and entered. What had he been doing there? I was sure that he planned some type of mischief for me.

I was carrying a small dark lanthorn to light my way down the ladder. Raising the slide, I exposed the candle and used the flame to light the larger lanthorn in my cabin. With that light, I started to search my room. I wondered at first if he had taken anything, but soon discovered that nothing seemed to be missing. I then thought that he might have planted something, like an empty rum bottle, in the room to get me in trouble with the captain. I found nothing missing and nothing added. Perkins must have been snooping. I was sure of this when I opened the rosewood box that held the sextant. I always put the instrument away with the arm exactly on the thirty-degree mark. It's almost a compulsion to do so. The pointer now was on the twenty-eight-degree division. I closed the case and put it back in my sea chest. I didn't know what Mr. Midshipman Perkins had been doing in my cabin, but I didn't like it, not at all.

Two days after leaving Spithead, we sighted a sail. Recognition signals were run up the halliards and answered. We had found the fleet. Whenever a new ship joins the fleet, it is the cause for rejoicing. New ships bring fresh provisions and mail. We were the replacement for a 74 that had sprung a mast cap. She was to sail for home to refit while we took her place in the blockading line. We would sail about in easy reach of the French fleet anchorage. Either they would remain penned in the harbor, or if they decided to come out in force, we would engage them. I didn't think that there was much chance of a fleet action. When France had fallen to the Revolutionaries, many of her senior naval officers were of noble blood. Those that did not escape to England were executed. The Directory of France did not have enough senior officers to man the fleet.

We took our station near the flagship, a second-rater of ninety-eight guns, which was flying a broad pennant. The flags rising to the three-decker's masthead spelled out our number. The captain was ordered to report to the admiral. As Gamble's gig was swung out and lowered, more signal flags ascended skyward. They were signaling to the fleet that mail had arrived. Our captain's gig pulled away toward the flagship, its oars biting the water with perfect tempo. Even as he left, we could see a myriad of small boats, some under sail, others pulled by oar; they were heading toward us. Every ship in the fleet had sent a boat to pick up their mail and whatever fresh food we could spare. By the time the last of them had left, the captain himself was skimming over the water. He had made his presence known and delivered the dispatches to the admiral. Now he was coming back and we aboard the *Monmouth* would take up the job the Admiralty had sent us to do.

Blockading, especially in February, is difficult work. It was no easier in March or the first week of April. Spring had come, or so the calendar said, but I had seen no green blades of grass, smelled no flowers, nor heard the song of a robin. One day melded into the next with precise uniformity. The days so alike you could stack them in a pile. Blockading is monotonous work; tempers are on edge and get more so each day as the food spoils, the water grows a zoo of animal life, and the ship seems to be disintegrating. We needed a refit, but instead of returning to England, we kept station with the other ships, each as badly off as we.

If the water kegs had been scoured out properly, the water would still be good. Someone had blundered and it was necessary to strain the thick green liquid through cloth before it could be swallowed. The ship's bread also teemed with animal life. Tapping the biscuits against the table brought the weevils. The black-headed weevils and the pale green coachmen, came wiggling out like snakes, looking angry at being displaced from their home.

Despite the weather, the foul water, the bad food, we continued our daily routine. I was on duty in the second half of the dog watch. Seven bells were struck, signifying a half hour before the watches would change. The off-duty crew members came up on deck and went into formation for church service. It was time for the daily torture; worse for me than for some, for I would have to hear the sermon twice. Once while I held the deck, and again when my watch attended the second service. Our chaplain, Mr. Oates, was a fire-breathing Methodist. With only half an hour before the formation would be dismissed, he tried to cram as much hellfire and damnation into those thirty minutes as my former Anglican dominie delivered in a year. The format of the service was inflexible. First a hymn was called for; the men lifted raucous voices in song, aware of informers taking the names of those who did not sing. If one of the "deacons" took a man's name, it could cost him his liquor ration. With the last doleful echo gone, Oates would launch into a sermon against fornication. He spoke so long and so loudly and with such great detail about fornication that he would inevitably remind me of my chaste status. After hearing him preach, I positively hungered for a woman. After the fornication, we were served with another hymn followed by a diatribe against drinking and chewing tobacco. The captain then might add a few choice words of his own; they were always the same words. Time was running out; we had all been consigned to a burning hell for our sins; the smell of brimstone was heavy on the upper deck. The chaplain would then lead us in the closing hymn as the bell pealed eight times, ending the second dog watch. Those who had been working would now line up in formation to be served up a platter full of fornication, drinking, and tobacco.

It was rather comical in a way. Every day we were bombarded with the Lord's message about fornication, drinking, and the evils of tobacco, but the seamen were all given their ration of beer and rum every day. Each man including the officers received a gallon of beer. Since the officers had been coerced into signing away their spirits, we had no hard liquor; the men were still served theirs. A healthy fear of a bloody uprising prevented the captain from doing more to the crew than telling them about the evils of Demon Rum. He did water the men's spirits more than other ships, but not enough for them to complain. Instead of cutting the 190-proof rum with two parts of water, he used three. Each man received a daily half-pint of the diluted rum. I think the captain used the money he saved from the extra dilution of the drink to pay for the printing of the religious tracts he handed out to the men.

Tobacco was considered essential to their well-being by most seamen. It was medicine, food, and drink. No effort was made to limit its use. As far as fornication was concerned, no one was in immediate danger of damnation from that cause. We carried no women aboard the *Monmouth*, though other king's ships did so. The only chance a seaman had to become a sinner was in port. Although the men were seldom if ever allowed ashore, any woman claiming to be a seaman's wife would be allowed aboard when the ship was at anchor in a harbor. The women were never questioned. Were we to sail to China, Chinese women would have been allowed on board if they first claimed to be wives. Fortunately for the men, the whores in every port were well aware of this custom and invariably made the claim.

The religious tracts were distributed to every man aboard

ship, even those who were illiterate. Human nature can't be changed by tracts or by preaching, but the chaplain and the captain kept trying. The whole process was offensive to me. I have never cared to have another chap tell me, "My doxy is orthodoxy, yours is heterodoxy."

Chapter 3

Mr. Midshipman Sparrshott turned the half-hour glass and signaled to the marine waiting on the fo'c'sle to strike the ship's bell. The dulcet notes rang out boldly, audible throughout the ship from cable tier to masthead. The eight bells ended the forenoon watch; it was once again twelve o'clock, noon. I relieved Hallowell of the watch and took over the ship. When the bell sounded, the old nautical day ended and a new one started, for seamen use the solar day. It was still April 9 ashore, but afloat it was now April 10. I thought that Mr. Sparrshott was no longer on duty, but all the midshipmen were to shoot the sun. He lingered on the quarterdeck, watching the grains of sand trickle through the small aperture of the half-hour glass. As he watched, he sniffed deeply and wiped his nose on his sleeve.

The sun was nearly to its zenith now; it was time to make the sighting. Under the watchful eyes of Mr. Grimstead, the master, all of the midshipmen raised their sextants. The quarterdeck was crowded, for the first and second lieutenants were making the official sighting. Not wishing to be left out, I raised my sextant and brought the sun down to sit on the horizon line. I read the inclination off the engraved arm and awaited confirmation from the other officers. While waiting, I checked my watch, which I had just set by the chronometer. For every fifteen degrees of longitude, there is an hour's change in time. Fifteen degrees west is an hour earlier; fifteen degrees east is an hour later. The watch, which was set to Greenwich time, disagreed with the sun time by reading twenty minutes later. That meant that the chronometer was keeping good time, for here off Brest and Ushant we were five degrees west of London and Greenwich. The others were finished with their calculations. They agreed on the latitude with me, but some of the midshipmen seemed to be having difficulties, judging from the tone of the master's voice.

Grimstead chased the youngsters off to their other duties, but remained on deck to keep watch over me. Captain Gamble still didn't trust me alone with the ship, so the master was assigned to act as my guardian angel. Hallowell had told me that for the first six months he too had to have a shepherd.

The wind was moderate, about nine knots; the sky pale azure where it could be seen between the billowy cumulus. Periodically a fat white cloud drifted between us and the weak sun, darkening the deck of the *Monmouth*. I was watching the effect of the wind on the sails; ready to perfect them to take advantage of the wind direction if need be. I noticed that the sails had bellied out hard and taut. The wind was freshening. "Mr. Grimstead," I said, "it's freshening a bit. Should we inform the captain?"

The master put a finger in his mouth to wet it; holding the finger up to the air stream, he pondered my question. Grimstead was a tiny man, standing barely five feet in his sea boots. He looked frail enough for the freshening wind to blow him overboard, but he had been a seaman for thirty years. He was a real bucko type, probably as a result of his short stature. He was called "Grim Grimstead" behind his back by all the common seamen. "I thing we can wait for maybee 'arf an 'our longer, sir," he said, "but if it starts to freshen a mite more, we'ud better call the capting."

The wind velocity continued to increase; it grew cold on the wind-swept quarterdeck, making me thankful for my warm pea jacket. Just before three bells, I called for the captain. He shot out from his day cabin just below the quarterdeck, looked around, sniffed twice with that enormous nose, and said, "Mr. St. John, have a couple of reefs taken in the tops'ls." He turned and scuttled back down the ladder to his cabin, looking like a giant blue and gold cockroach. That was fine with me; I much preferred not to have him watch over me. I had quite enough of the captain at each morning prayer service. I continued to pace up and down on the quarterdeck, watching the masthead pennants and the courses. If the wind were to veer, we could be taken aback; the first indication would be a change in the direction of the flags flying at the mast tops. Far off, almost directly on the port horizon, I became aware of a small patch of black cloud contrasting violently with the fluffy cumulus. It was a long distance away, for it looked no bigger than Mr. Lloyd's dog. "Mr. Grimstead!" I shouted.

With a quick, shuffling gait, he came to where I was standing, shielded his eyes with one palm, and stared intently at the spot. Spitting out his cud of tobacco, he said, "Trouble brewing there, I things, sir. Yer'd bess call the capting afore it 'its us."

I passed the word for the captain, sending Mr. Roderick Sparrshott, one of the midshipmen, as my messenger. Sparrshott was an undernourished-looking, pimply-faced specimen. His father was a wealthy ship's chandler, a self-made man, but poor Sparrshott was too stupid to pour sea water out of a boot. He should have been off watch, but was serving an extra period for some sin or infraction he had committed. He was my cross to bear during this watch; I only hoped that we would have no signals to send, for Sparrshott would be sure to snag the halliards and get the messages all bollocksed. To put it kindly, young Sparrshott didn't know his arse from the sounding well. For a farthing, I would have gladly pitched him over the side of the ship, content to have done a good deed. The midshipman blanched when I told him to fetch the captain, blanched as white as an unbaked plum duff. For a second I thought he might protest, but discipline won out over fear and he took to his heels as if possessed.

"Yes, Mr. St. John." It was Captain Gamble.

I said nothing; I just pointed toward the black spot that was growing larger as we moved parallel to it. At last I spoke. "There, sir."

"Ah, yes," said Gamble. "Prepare to wear ship."

Picking up a tin speaking trumpet, I shouted, "Prepare to wear ship!" The single order was enough. Topmen sprang to the weather shrouds and started clambering aloft. The wind, much fresher now, molded their bodies into the substance of the ropes. Had anyone been foolish enough to climb the lee shrouds, he would have been blown into the sea. The wind slowed the men's ascent; they continued to claw their way upward, ever upward, pausing only when the gusts of wind were too great to climb, until they reached the great yards and made their way out to the yard ends on the foot ropes while clutching the canvas sails. Aloft, it's one hand for yourself and one hand for the ship.

The freshening winds had made waves, ever larger waves, which pounded at the liner. The action of the waves made the masts gyrate through the air in a swirling, looping pattern that could make a man dizzy to watch. As masts, yards, sails, and topmen undulated through space, I watched them. saying, "Better they than me," under my breath. I shuddered at the very thought of climbing up that gossamer tracery of lines until I was over one hundred fifty feet above the water. If I couldn't have terra firma, give me the quarterdeck.

The topmen sent the tops'ls and topmasts down as the ship wore in a large arc and headed off at right angles to where she had been going. The cloud was moving faster than we were; it caught up with us. The sun was blacked out, making it seem as if dusk had fallen; it started to rain heavy drops that hit the deck and seemed to bounce upward on impact. The force of these raindrops stung when they hit me, even through my pea jacket and uniform. This did not last long, for the main body of the cloud was now directly overhead sheeting water upon us; individual drops could no longer be discerned. I didn't have my tarpaulin coat or hat; I was drenched by the downpour.

The wind of the storm had raised ever increasing waves, vast waves of water that threatened to engulf the ship, swallowing us like the whale did Jonah, but since we were running with the storm, the wind was at our stern and the waves were moving in the same direction we were. Had we not worn the ship, they would have come crashing over the side to inundate us. As it was, we did not escape scot-free; the following waves were moving faster than the ship. As each hit us, it would lift the stern of the *Monmouth* high into the air; as the wave passed beneath the keel, the liner would drop with a sickening twist into the trough only to rise again with the next wave and repeat the performance.

I had to admire the captain's seamanship. If we had not veered away from the storm, the waves would have been perpendicular to our line of travel. Hitting us abeam, they possibly could have broached the ship. By laying her before the wind, we were running with the storm and in no great danger. The storm had been raging for almost an hour. The captain was still on the quarterdeck. He, like me, had not put on his foul-weather gear. He stood there, as wet as I, looking older than God. From the expression on his face, I fully expected him to raise his fist skyward and demand of his Maker that the storm cease, but he did no such thing. I realized at last that he was exultantly praying. What I thought of as anger was ecstasy; he was pleased to have God test him.

Mr. Sparrshott was standing near me on the lee side of the quarterdeck, leaving the captain the privacy of the weather side. He was neither damper nor more miserable-looking than either the captain or I, but his pimply face was a pale shade of green. He gasped and choked, then ran for the rail. The corkscrew motion of the ship was too much for his stomach. Sparrshott reached the bulwark and spewed up whatever he had eaten.

Mr. Grimstead, the master, was on the quarterdeck too. He seemed totally unconcerned at the gale. He had his legs braced well apart and rode each pitch of the ship with great aplomb. Maybe he was built too close to the deck for the wind to disturb. As I watched him, he reached into a pocket and pulled out a plug of navy cut; slicing off a piece with a battered clasp knife, he popped it into his mouth and started chewing. The captain flashed him a dirty look when he saw the tobacco, but said nothing.

The rain started to let up; the cloud was moving faster than the *Monmouth*; it passed us, taking the wind and the rain with it. "Hoist the mains'ls, Mr. St. John," said the captain as he went below to change into dry clothing. I pulled my watch out and looked at it. There was still an hour left of my watch; I would remain wet and uncomfortable until I was relieved.

Chapter 4

The day was fair, fair and pleasant after a week of incessant rain and cold. The cerulean dome of the sky was unmarred by clouds, looking much like a vast Sistine Chapel roof before Michelangelo started his labors. The sun, a hot, bright, incandescent sun, beat its welcome warmth down on the sea. The *Monmouth* was hove to by the wind; no anchor had been dropped, but reversed yards on the foremast allowed the ship to overcome the pressure of the wind on the main and mizzen sails. The water was still, unmarred by wavelets; it reflected a mirror image of the two-decker to be admired by anyone leaning over the rail. Other ships of the fleet were in sight in both directions, while still others were just over the horizon. These invisible ships were linked to those visible by a signaling system perfected during the late American war. Each ship could see at least one other. When signals were flown, each repeated the message for the next ship down the line. In that way each captain could be kept informed of any and all developments. With the aid of the signal system, the fleet formed a continuous fence, preventing the French from breaking out unnoticed.

I was standing on the quarterdeck of the *Monmouth;* it was my watch, but I was not alone. The captain was pacing back and forth on the weather side and muttering something under his breath. The ship was heeled over on the port tack, giving him the look of a man who had one leg shorter than the other. I watched him and thought that he might be practicing some new remarks for the next church service. If so, any change would be welcomed. I was getting rather bored with the constant repetition. On my side of the deck, Mr. Lloyd, our first lieutenant, stood near the taffrail, looking elegant and vacuous as he gazed off into space. We were rather crowded on the lee side while the captain had the entire weather side to himself. In addition to myself and Mr. Lloyd, the master, Mr. Grimstead, and a whole gaggle of midshipmen were present; he was instructing them in the art of navigation. Grimstead finished his class and dismissed them; all the midshipmen but one followed the master down the ladder and left the quarter-deck.

Mr. Perkins, the captain's younger nephew, remained, for he was sharing my watch with me. He was acting as flag midshipman. He was competent enough to do this duty; the only thing that had prevented him from passing the lieutenant's examination was his mathematics. Competent or not, I didn't like the slug. I looked over the taffrail and watched the wake arrowing out behind the ship's stern for a few seconds. When I turned back, I saw Mr. Lloyd leaving the quarterdeck with the captain. His little brown spaniel did not follow him, but remained on the quarterdeck snuffling like crazy. The dog eventually nosed his way to Mr. Perkins, where he lifted his leg and drenched the midshipman's hose. Howling obscenities, Perkins kicked the beast. The spaniel hit the planking some eight feet away; yelping in pain, he jumped to the main deck to get away. The last I saw of the animal was his drooping tail as he scurried off, yipping loudly.

There are certain standards of deportment and decorum

that I try to follow. It wasn't proper to laugh at that little sod, Perkins, but I just couldn't control myself when that dog let fly. I burst out into a loud, almost braying laugh, but ceased as soon as the dog was kicked. I didn't say anything to Mr. Perkins about the dog; I figured that it was a family matter and left it to Mr. Lloyd to take any action he might think appropriate. Perkins was lucky that the captain had left, for if his cursing had been overheard, he would have been punished. As for myself, I was heartily ashamed that I had given vent to my feelings; if I were ever to become a captain, I would have to learn to control my emotions.

As I said before, I didn't like Perkins. He was a dreadful bully who made life for the younger midshipmen unadulterated hell. Today, what with his kicking the poor dog, I found him particularly loathsome, for I wasn't feeling well. I must have eaten some tainted food; much of what we had aboard was so foul that no spice could make it palatable. I had the chills so badly that I had not taken off my pea jacket even after the sun came out. My guts were in a turmoil; I couldn't wait for my watch to end so I could dash for the officer's head.

"Message coming in, sir," said Perkins. I looked at the nearest ship. Flags were blossoming out in the mastheads. Perkins was studying the flags through his telescope and referring to the code book. "To all ships," he said. "Captains to report to the flagship."

"Thank you, Mr. Perkins," I said. "Pass the word to the crew of the captain's gig and inform the captain." He left. I watched as the gig was swayed out over the side and lowered to the water. The captain came up from his cabin wearing a fresh uniform and a clean shave. Even a senior captain makes sure that he looks presentable before reporting to the admiral. Though Gamble didn't look as elegant as Mr. Lloyd, he was neat and clean.

The gig was waiting in the water at the side of the liner. It was being held fast by two men with boat hooks. I watched the captain scramble down the side and take his place in the stern sheets of the boat. His epaulettes were of real gold bullion, not brass; they reflected the sunlight back at me. I wondered as I watched about the wisdom of the Navy's adopting this French fashion shortly after the last war. As the only man aboard ship to wear epaulettes, the captain or commander was a marked man. The sharp-shooters in the enemy's fighting top would easily recognize the captain by this piece of ostentation. The old uniform, the plain blue coat, was less liable to attract attention. Thank God few muskets were true enough to hit a target, but I had learned that the American Navy was using rifles in their tops. Since we weren't at war with the Americans, that wasn't a problem, unless the French picked up that custom.

Gamble was seated now; he put his cocked hat on his head. It was a handsome cocked hat made of real beaver felt by one of London's best hatters. I didn't blame the captain for not wearing that hat while he went down the side of the ship. If ever I had enough money, I would like one just like it. The captain's cox'n gave an order; the gig's crew started to row, their long-bladed oars flashing in the sunlight. Just then, the marine struck the bell eight times; my watch was over; Mr. Hallowell reported to relieve me.

I left the poop with undecorous haste, dashing for the bow of the ship. The officer's head was unoccupied, thank God. I lifted the curtain and entered. I was none too soon; I just had time to get my arse across the bar when I erupted. "Praise the Lord," I muttered, sounding more like

the captain every day. It would have been most embarrassing for an officer of the king otherwise. Relieved, I searched
for some bum wipe, but to my consternation, I had none. I
was getting frantic as I went through every pocket. I finally
looked in the pockets of the pea jacket and found some
papers. Checking to see if they could be spared, I saw that
they were the religious tracts the captain had given me.
They were only printed on one side; I wouldn't smear ink
over my bum fiddle. Pulling up my breeches, I left the
head. As I lifted the curtain and stepped out, I almost
tripped over a seaman holystoning the deck directly in
front of the necessary. He was one of a working party supervised by the master-at-arms, Mr. Skuggs. The man working the prayer book against the deck looked up at me and
said, "Beg yer parding, sir, I 'opes yer didn' 'urt yerseff."

Bumping into someone as you leave the head is a little
demeaning. "Carry on," I said in a grand manner to cover
up my embarrassment. The man resumed his holystoning
and I went below to my quarters. Cramped as my little
cube was, it was pure luxury when compared to the lot of
the common seaman. Their hammock allowance is only
fourteen inches per man. This isn't as bad as it sounds, for
half the men are on duty while the other half sleep. Alternating hammock spaces by the watch actually gave each
man twenty-eight inches of room. I was still feeling queasy
and weak, so I dropped myself on the cot, curled into a
ball, and tried to sleep my sickness away.

I woke to the sound of knuckles rapping at the partition
of my cubicle. "Yes?" I said, dragging the back of my hand
across my sleep-drugged eyes.

"Capt'n Gamble wants t' see ya in his cabin, now!" It
was Mr. Midshipman Perkins. He had a strange, enigmatic
smile on his toadlike face that made him look as if he had
gotten into the captain's preserves. His bulging eyes glis-

tened with some emotion I couldn't name. Whatever it was, it gave him great satisfaction to fetch me. I watched as his tongue darted in and out between his lips; it seemed to hesitate, to be licking his chops in delight. This was so different from his usual whining behavior, I instantly realized that his cause for satisfaction meant trouble for me; knowing this, he was inordinately pleased.

"Dismissed, Mr. Perkins!" I told him. As I heard his footsteps recede, I poured some water from the pitcher into my washbasin. I washed the sleep out of my eyes and slipped into my best uniform coat. The breeches and hose I was wearing would have to do.

The sentry allowed me into the captain's day cabin. It was a huge place, for the entire width of the stern was devoted to his quarters. Unlike the blackness of the cockpit where the midshipmen live, or the gloom of a lieutenant's cabin, the captain's lodging was well lighted by sunlight streaming in through the huge stern windows. Beyond the thick glass, he had a private gallery, a seagoing balcony. The entire space, more than allotted to all the lieutenants, the midshipmen, and the warrant officers, was devoted to the ease and comfort of one man, the captain. The vast area was divided by partitions into a dining room, a day cabin, and two night cabins. Gamble had done himself proud in furnishing his quarters. A built-in couch curved with the stern of the boat, following the arc of the hull. Several upholstered chairs were bolted to the deck to prevent sliding each time the ship changed tack and heeled the other direction. The deck was covered with a large rectangular piece of Turkish carpeting and several smaller rugs. He even had a garden planted in several large wooden half barrels placed to receive the sunlight through the windows. The captain was seated behind a library table when I

entered. I came up to him and while standing at attention
said, "Lt. Sinjin reporting as directed, sir."

When I entered the cabin, he had a forefinger up one
nostril and was ferreting away, as he had been the last time
I was in his cabin. He said nothing until he completed the
task, but a display of colors played over his face changing it
from white to tomato aspic and then white again. At last
he removed his finger; wiping his prize off on the underside
of the table, he glared at me. The aurora-borealis-like display was over; his face was now as red if not redder than a
marine's uniform coat. He looked angry. As he stared, no,
glared, at me, he tried to say something, but nothing came
out. The wattles on his neck vibrated and I heard a hoarse
rattle. Finally he gasped out the word, "Blasphemer!" He
had found his voice. "Anti-Christ!" he screamed. "You, St.
John, are the devil's disciple!"

"Sir?" I said.

"Don't you deny it, St. John. I saw it with my own
eyes!"

"Saw what, sir?"

"Mr. St. John, you used the name of the Lord to wipe
your backside."

I almost laughed, but this was the captain. Aboard a
king's ship he was even mightier than God. He held the
power of life and death, the power of promotion. If for
some reason he took a dislike to an officer or man, he could
ruin him. I had always thought of that God figure, the captain, as an aloof, stern, paternal figure somewhat akin to
the Jehovah of the Old Testament. A man like Pellew fit
that picture. Gamble, the God figure aboard this ship, was
acting like a demented Jupiter ready to throw his thunder-
bolts to avenge what he considered an insult. I was un-
done. I did not answer him; whatever I said would only
make it worse.

BEFORE THE WIND 43

"Don't deny it, Mr. St. John. Skuggs saw you in the head when it happened. If the wind hadn't blown my hat off into the sea, you might have gotten away with your crime; I would have been away from the ship. While we were fishing my hat from the water, you committed your dastardly deed and I saw the sheets flutter down from the head." As he spoke, I noticed his hat; that beautiful beaver-felt cocked hat; it looked as limp and matted as a drowned dog. It lay on one end of the table in a small pool of water. The captain was still speaking. I forced myself to concentrate on what he was saying. "I found the literature, the despoiled literature, in the water, St. John. God intended that I catch you at your unspeakably filthy crime, or my hat would not have blown off at that time. I don't know what I shall do with you. If I could, I would keelhaul you, but that is no longer allowed. Consider yourself under arrest and confined to your quarters, except for mealtimes. Mr. Perkins will take over your duties."

Dismissed, I left his cabin and headed back to my own. I was in trouble, real trouble. Although there was no clause in the Articles of War that made my offense subject to a court-martial, not even the last article, the catch-all section, I was still in trouble. If a captain wants to crucify an officer, sooner or later he will find an opportunity. The only thing I could do was stay on my best behavior in hopes that if no immediate grounds for court-martial were given to the captain, he would have me transferred just to get rid of me.

Chapter 5

The cabin was cramped, close, and claustrophobic, but at least I had some measure of privacy. As I wouldn't have duty the next watch or the watch after, I undressed and went to bed. I could use the sleep, but it wouldn't come. I lay there twisted up on that too short cot and listened to the groaning sounds of the ship's timbers, to the song of the wind in the rigging, to the pattering sounds of horny bare feet flapping against the deck; I lay there and felt sorry for myself. Was it so black a crime I had committed? Captain Gamble would flay me if he could and have my hide tanned to cover the ship's drums. At last I dropped into a fitful, troubled sleep, but I was aware of each time the bell was struck, aware of the change of watch, aware of each tack in the ship's direction. The *Monmouth* now heeled over to the other side; we were sailing on the larboard, I should say port, tack. We were sailing away from Ushant, away from Brest. I wondered where we were heading.

The next day, the captain must have reconsidered my position, I was returned to duty. From the sharp looks he gave me and the constant presence of either Skuggs or one of his other toadies, I wasn't forgiven or forgotten. I think he had decided to give me enough rope to allow me to tie my own noose. If so, I wasn't in any hurry to oblige him.

We were sailing south along the coast of France when I came up on deck. I looked around to see if other ships of our fleet were with us. We seemed to be alone; the second officer confirmed this when I asked. Faced with the constant shortage of frigates, the admiral had dispatched the *Monmouth*, the weakest of his liners, to do a frigate's work. While the 74's continued to hold the French fleet in the harbor at Brest, we had been assigned to independent duty. The thought of possible prize money was not enough to relax my fear of what the captain had planned for me. I would have been delighted to resign my commission, but the subject never came up. I did my best not to think of my problems, but the rare looks the captain shot my way as he walked the quarterdeck continually brought them to mind. The only consolation for my predicament was that I had been asked not to attend church services. Rather than save my soul, the captain must have confined me to hell and perdition, denying me the sacrament and salvation. It was not nice to be considered a pariah, but it did have the compensation of not having to stand in formation and listen to that windy oaf, Chaplain Oates. My watch completed, I turned the deck over to my replacement and descended the ladder to my quarters. Two seamen were in my cabin painting the cheeks of the 24-pounder carriage a blood hiding, bright red. Because blood does not show on red, it is a much favored color for gun port covers and gun carriages. The air in the tiny cube was filled with the choking fumes of fresh paint; I wouldn't be able to stay there; the stench in that tiny airless space would make me sick.

"Hsstt, sir," said one of the men, placing a finger across his lips. I recognized him; his name was Morris, Horace Morris. Appropriately enough for a gunner's mate, his round head was totally bald, looking like a huge, skin-covered cannon ball. He was a Canadian from Halifax if I remembered correctly. His companion was less familiar; I searched my memory for his name. It wasn't too hard to dredge up, for the man was a redheaded, freckle-faced Irishman. Murphy was the name; he was one of the waisters. "Sir," said Morris, "we just wants you t' know that we're wit you."

"Yass, by Jasus, I'm sairtain that the good fayther woulda say that it's no sin to put Methodist literature to its proper use, sair," said the Irishman.

There is an old saying in the Navy: "Today's wardroom joint is tomorrow's fo'c'sle stew." What was said by the officers would soon be rehashed by the men. I laughed at Murphy's remark. He was a Catholic of course, and felt out of place on a Protestant ship. Seamen were in short supply, such short supply that His Majesty's forces pressed all despite their religion. Catholics, Muslims, Jews, and even idol worshipers could be found serving on king's ships. It made no difference if a seaman were white, black, brown, or yellow; it made no difference if he were born in England, Ireland, Germany, Sweden, India, Africa, the United States, or even in France. Once a man had been pressed, he was a jolly tar, a British Jack. If a man were not of English birth and Protestant religion, it would be as difficult for him to become an officer as it was for the rich man in the biblical parable to enter the kingdom of heaven; but when it came to holystoning the decks, hauling the braces, climbing the rigging, or working the guns, the Jew, the Catholic, the yellow man, the black man were good enough. It must have really rankled a devout Catholic to be forced to stand and listen to a Methodist sermon every day. I could understand the rancor in Murphy's voice.

"Thank you, gentlemen," I said to them and left my cabin. I could have stayed in the wardroom, but since all of the lieutenant's cabins open into the wardroom, the smell of paint was heavy there too. Instead, I went back on deck where the air would be fresh and pure. The gun carriage could have been painted at another time. Obviously the captain or his minions weren't above petty harassment.

We continued to sail south. I was still in Coventry, but at least the weather remained nice and I had a chance to commune with myself. At mess in the wardroom, the only officer who would speak to me was John Gamble, the second lieutenant. Hallowell did manage to catch me alone and apologize for snubbing me when others were present; he was fearful that if he were civil to me Lieutenant Lloyd would report him to the captain. Big John Gamble didn't give a damn what his uncle, the captain, thought. I think he wanted to annoy him, for he even spoke to me when the captain was present. I wasn't happy with the situation, for it was strained and uncomfortable.

As we continued our cruise, we sailed past Belle-Île, past the Île d'Yeu, the Île de Ré, and the Île d'Orléan. The seas were quiet; we saw no other ships except for a few fishing vessels. It was against policy to bother fishermen. The only one we stopped sold us some fish and swore that he had not seen other ships. Since he was a Frenchman, we assumed that he lied to us. This was confirmed not half an hour later when we sighted a sail. "Sail ho!" shouted the lookout.

We gave chase immediately. It was shortly after noon; we had shot the latitude just before we sighted the ship. My reading at noon placed us at 45°33′ North. At that point, the coast of France is a solid wall unbroken by any inlets or harbors. The closest place of refuge lies just north at the entrance of the Gironde estuary. Unfortunately for the ship we were chasing, the *Monmouth* blocked the way to the north. The quarry was forced to sail south where the next harbor was the Arcachon Basin. That was a good forty-five miles in a straight line, but since the land mass at Cape Ferret had to be rounded, they couldn't sail in a straight line for sea room was needed to get around the cape.

"Set out the stuns'ls!" shouted the captain. The topmen went aloft to lay booms out from the yards and hoist the steering sails. The wind was directly abeam, to our starboard side. The *Monmouth* heeled over to port and as the enlarged area of canvas was pulled taut by the wind increased her speed. Although I could not see it, I knew that the liner had a bone in her teeth, the bow roiling up the water as we boiled along. For an old lady, the two-decker was making *beaucoup* knots. The other ship was moving quickly too. If only we had been a frigate instead of this lubberly tub, the prize would be ours. It was a ship-rigged vessel of at least 450 tons burthen. Deep laden as she was, we almost caught her, but it was too short a chase for the *Monmouth* to close the gap completely. We did gain ground; as the chase went between Cape Ferret and Arcachon point, we were not over four cable lengths or half a nautical mile away. At that distance, we were in gun range, but unless something vital were hit there was little chance of stopping the ship. "Fire the bow chaser! Fire her high, at the mast," shouted the captain.

The 9-pounder in the eyes of the boat went off with a loud crack and recoiled its ton and a half weight against the breeching tackle. A cloud of dense, white smoke hung over the fo'c'sle as the men swabbed the bore, reloaded the gun, and pushed it out through the gun port again. The stench of the discharged powder hung in the air over the ship's bow. Seconds later the stern of the liner was passing where the beak had been and the acrid, brimstone fumes were strong in my nostrils. The gun fired again; once more I heard the thin, spiteful crack of the 9-pounder, so unlike the roar of a 24. I thought for a second that we were going to follow the ship into the anchorage, but French guns mounted on either headland opened fire on us. A ball passed through the main course, splitting the great sail as neatly as a pair of shears. While there was still time to wear, the captain did so. We came about, still under fire, but now our batteries opened on the forts. When I was restored to duty, I had been placed in charge of the 9-pounders on the quarterdeck. I could feel the planking below me shake as the 18's on the gun deck opened up followed by the 24's on the lower deck. There were enemy batteries on either side of us; we fired both broadsides. The massed explosion of so many guns shook the two-decker, wrenching the timbers and fabric, but it was built to withstand such punishment. Great gouts of smoke arose from the muzzles of the guns and permeated the entire ship. It was hard to breathe. As each gun recoiled, its wildly screaming crew sponged it out and reloaded to fire again and again.

We were now out of range of the land batteries. The order to secure guns was given. I wondered if the French fire had killed any of our men or damaged the ship beyond what I could see. It had all happened so quickly that I had not had the time to be frightened, but now that it was over, the familiar gut-wrenching churning of my stomach told me that I could have been killed or mutilated. I sheathed the cutlass that I had drawn to give the firing orders to my gun crews and waited for further orders. As I waited, I looked around, searching for damage. One of the enemy balls had cut a furrow across the planks of the quarterdeck, passing close to where I had stood. It had missed the 9-pounder by as narrow a margin as it missed me and skipped across the deck to crash into the bulwark at the other side. When it hit the bulwark, it had sent a shower of splinters, long, jagged, lethal splinters, into the nearby gun crew. One man lay on the deck, a two-foot-long piece of oak through his throat; he was dead. Two others were in the cockpit to have splinters removed. Thank God for the fact that oak splinters seldom leave a festering wound. If they had been teak, the injuries would be sure to be infected.

The quarterdeck is no place to be during a fire fight, I realized. When I had been put in charge of the 9-pounders instead of my regular position on the first gun deck, I had thought that Gamble was trying to humiliate me by having me do midshipman's work while he let Perkins take charge of my 18-pounders. Now I began to wonder if he had other than humiliation in his mind. Perhaps he was trying to expose me to more danger in hopes that my mutilation or death would resolve his problem.

Disappointed at the loss of a rich prize, we sailed back to the open sea. "Heave to!" shouted the captain. The waisters grabbed the braces and hauled the foresails round; the *Monmouth* came to rest. We were hove to just out of sight of Cape Ferret. The captain called Mr. Lloyd and Mr. John Gamble to his cabin for a conference. Hallowell and I were excluded. I was surprised that the third was not included, for that would have been another way to annoy me. Fifteen minutes later, the three men reappeared on deck. The captain motioned Hallowell and me to join them. A reprieve, I thought, but I was soon disillusioned. "I am sending a cutting-out party to take that ship," said the captain. "Mr. St. John will lead the expedition. He will take the cutter."

"But, sir," said Hallowell, "I am senior to Mr. St. John."

"I am well aware of that fact, Mr. Hallowell, but seniority has nothing to do with this; if it had, Mr. Lloyd is senior to all of the other lieutenants." I could see Lloyd open his mouth to speak, but a look from the captain silenced him. Senior or not, Gamble wouldn't trust Lloyd to walk a dog much less lead an expedition. The man for the job was Lieutenant John Gamble, but the old man wouldn't expose him to any risk. That was one of the reasons the lieutenant hated his uncle. If he were never exposed to a chance for glory, he might never be posted captain. That left Hallowell and me. If there were to be glory, I couldn't see him choosing me. No, he expected trouble and thought that I was the most expendable of his officers. He was probably praying that I wouldn't return. His next words made a certainty of my suspicion that his motive was ulterior. "Only one boat will go in, Mr. St. John's boat. We will be here waiting for you to bring the ship out, Mr. St. John."

Despite knowing what the sanctimonious old bastard planned, I was almost flattered by his seeming confidence until I saw the list of the men who were to go with me. Morris, the Canadian, Murphy, the Irishman, along with six of his Catholic countrymen, Singh, the Hindu, Goldman, the Jew, and Hadad, the Mussulman, were in my crew. These men and some of the others I recognized as being on the captain's black list. These were the men the captain's toadies caught not singing or profaning the Sabbath. These were the men whose loss would put Gamble into that paradise he so demanded—the master of a Christian ship, or more exactly a Methodist ship. It seemed to me a most un-Christ-like way for a professed Christian to act, but mine was not to reason why; I had to follow orders, but I still had the prerogative of how to follow them. The one thing I knew was that I didn't have the chance of an icicle in Hades of being successful unless I could influence the odds. There were several hours left before darkness when we would embark on our expedition. I decided to spend that time getting some special equipment together.

Chapter 6

Night had fallen; despite a half moon, it was dark, darker than the pit of hell to which Chaplain Oates was continually consigning the souls of the sinners aboard the ship. This seemingly contradictory situation of Stygian blackness and moonlight could be explained by the dense, low mist that clung to the water, hiding its surface from the deck of the *Monmouth*. The special equipment I wanted for the expedition had been assembled by Morris, the gunner's mate. I watched closely as several tons of cutter were swung out over the rail to disappear into the mist. I imagined it being lowered into the water. The men who made up the cutting-out party went over the rail, disappearing as the thick fog enshrouded them. Taking a small musette bag with me, I followed them down into the cutter. Morris had put three barrels, three half barrels, of gunpowder and the slow match in the stern where I would sit. I smiled when I saw them; I didn't think that Captain Gamble was aware of their presence on the cutter.

At my command, the men started to row toward the headland. Someone had been efficient and taken care of a vital detail I had forgotten. The oars had been padded with rags dipped in slush from the galley. These muffled any squeaks or groans. If we were silent on the long row into the harbor, we had a chance to take the ship. Getting in was no problem; the problem would be in sailing the ship past the two batteries. If the fog persisted, it would be a tremendous help. "Who greased the oarlocks?" I asked.

"Me, sir," whispered back one of the men. It was Horace Morris.

"Good show, Morris."

"Thank you, sir. Sir, do we got a chanct of gettin' back?"

I was amazed at the perception of this question. It wasn't just me. "What do you mean?" I asked.

Morris didn't answer; Murphy did. "We're on a sooey-cide mission, ain't we, sair?"

"Not if we pull it off, Murphy."

"But, sair, how kin we pull it off, wit only one boat? By Jasus, that cantin' Methodist devil will be the death o' Mrs. Murphy's son Michael."

"If I had sent this cutting-out party, men, I would have sent three boats; we have only the one, so we will have to make up with guile what we lack in force." We had traveled about half the distance from the ship to the headland. "Rest on your oars," I told my men. As we rested, I opened the small bag and passed out some containers filled with a mixture of slush and soot from the galley stovepipe. "Smear this on your faces. We're going to board looking like blackamoors."

The men smeared the blacking over their faces. Although I could not see the bow of the cutter, those near me were given a satanic look. One of the containers made its way back to me so I applied the paste to my face. "Cor, sir," said one of the men, "yer looks like the de'il that preacher man is allus talkin' 'bout."

That would be all to the good. If we could produce fear in the crew of the ship we were boarding, half of our battle would be won in advance. I acted confident and brave for the men's sake, but inside I was a mass of calf's foot gelatin. Murphy was right; it was a suicide mission. The captain might have written the end to Mrs. St. John's son John too. Stiff upper lip and all that, I thought. I had to lead these poor sods into battle. The better the job I did, the better their chance of returning to rejoin their shipmates. If every man knew what he was expected to do once he was aboard the enemy ship, we would be organized while the crew of the ship were confused. I explained what I expected of each of them; they were each given a specific task and were expected to do it regardless of opposition. There would be no need to shout orders; we all knew exactly what to do. My cool demeanor must have had an effect on the men, for they all seemed confident, so confident that they gave me courage. I was pleased, for confidence is worth more than sheer animal bravery. We seemed ready now, as ready as ever we would be. That damned Captain Gamble; called himself a Christian, did he. He was about as Christian as Nero. Even if these men aboard the cutter did not agree with Gamble's religious beliefs, he had no right to throw away their lives. I was getting angry now, angry enough to lose my fear. I reached into the musette bag again and pulled out some strips of white rag. "Tie one around each of your heads so we'll be able to recognize each other."

"Beggin' yer pardon, sair, but you didn' put a rag 'roun' yer knob," said Murphy.

I was so carried away trying to get them ready that I had forgotten about myself. "Thank you, Murphy," I said as I knotted the rag around my head. I had to take off my cocked hat to do so. Since the hat would cover the rag and hide my identifying mark, I placed the hat on the stern seat next to me instead of returning it to my head. "We'll need a sign and a countersign," I said. "I think we'll use St. George as the sign. Can anyone suggest a good countersign?"

"The dragon," muttered one man.

"St. Patrick," said Murphy.

"That'll do," I said. "The sign is St. George, the answer St. Patrick. When you get aboard that ship, I want you to start screaming like banshees. The louder you shout, the more you'll frighten the Frenchies. We will use only cold steel; no guns, absolutely no guns, I'll keelhaul the man who disobeys that order. We'll take the ship and sail it out; we'll surprise Captain Gamble." We started to row again. I gave the men one last admonition. "From here on in until we board the ship, no talking!"

Thank God it was a misty night; the moonlight was almost completely blocked. A small boat with no sail is difficult to see on any night. With the fog, we would be invisible. We had a good chance to reach our objective without alerting the enemy. Thinking about how Captain Gamble was willing to throw away the lives of thirty-two seamen and an officer made me boil. I couldn't wait to attack the prize and rejoin the *Monmouth*. I would show that damned Gamble.

Someone nudged my arm; it was Morris. The man in the bow had sighted the ship. Mindful of my request for silence, he had sent back the information by body language. We were rowing more slowly now, trying to keep the noise level down. Would the anchor watch on the French ship hear us? The chains at the bow were now in sight; the seaman in the bow of the cutter hooked onto the chains with his boat hook; according to plan, six of my men started to climb up the chains to silence the anchor watch. The rest of us rowed around to the stern where we made the cutter fast to the ship. "I need a dependable man for boatkeeper," I whispered. Horace Morris was seated near me. "You, Morris," I said.

"I'd rather go with you, sir."

"Murphy?"

"By Jasus, sair, do ye mean to ask me t' miss a fight?"

"Then who?"

"Singh, sir," said Morris, pointing to one of the men. Singh, who was Hindu, refused to be converted to Christianity. That was probably why he had been sent with us.

I motioned to the Lascar and he worked his way back to the stern sheets of the cutter. When I took a better look at his short, slight stature, I knew that the man would be of more use here than boarding. We were ready to leave now. "Let's go get them, boys," I said, and we started up the stern of the ship. As we reached the top, I looked over the taffrail. The quarterdeck was almost deserted except for a single officer who was staring out toward the fo'c'sle. Morris and Murphy slipped up behind him; as Morris struck the man on the head, Murphy caught his sagging body and gently lowered it to the deck. We were all aboard; cutlasses and axes in hand, we moved forward and started to scream wildly.

The din was almost unbearable. It was as if every banshee and goblin that ever haunted a churchyard plus all of the imps and devils from hell were let loose aboard ship. The door of the French captain's cabin flew open; it had been thrown open and struck against a partition with a resounding rap. The cabin lamps threw a wide beam of light out onto the deck. Standing in the door, well illuminated by the light behind his back, stood a large man wearing a long nightshirt and a tasseled cap. He held a brace of pistols and was just thumbing back the hammers when I saw him. I rushed toward him to silence him as he ran up the ladder to the quarterdeck. I was not fast enough; he discharged one of the pistols directly at me, but for some reason missed. His eyes had probably not accommodated to the darkness on deck. As he raised the other pistol to have another go at me, a wild, eerie scream transfixed him for a second and then there was a flash of light reflecting off a boarding ax. Murphy had reached him before I could and had buried the pointed end of his ax in the man's skull, cutting right through the tasseled night cap.

The shot alerted whatever garrison there was near the ship. I could hear a rough voice screaming in French for his *enfants* to hurry, *sacrebleu!* These words were followed by the rattle of musketry. A few balls whistled through the rigging, but by then the mainsails were hauled into place and we were cutting the anchor cable. The sound of the ax against the cable was almost as loud but more welcome than gun shots from shore.

The howling, screaming, black-faced devils who had invaded the ship and killed their captain terrified the Frenchmen. They laid down their weapons and were locked below. I counted as the French seaman were put in the hold; there were only twenty-three of them and we were thirty-two. Maybe Gamble wasn't trying to sacrifice us when he sent only one boat in to cut out the prize. The ship was not a man-of-war or a privateer. Still, how could the captain be sure that she carried only a small crew.

The prize was ours. With all the sails shaken out, the land breeze filled them. The thunk of the ax was still heard at the bitts and the ship strained against the cable. A loud shout of delight from the bow was followed by a lurch of the ship as it parted company from the anchor. We were moving now, moving away from the muskets firing at us from the shore, moving toward the two batteries of heavy cannon on the headlands. I still worried about passing the gauntlet of the batteries, but having taken the ship I was

filled with confidence; it was not the false confidence I had
pretended to when we had left the *Monmouth;* it was
more a feeling of accomplishment. I couldn't afford to be
too cocksure. We still could be killed; the pistol shot followed by several volleys of musketry was sure to have
alerted the French soldiers in the fortifications. By the time
we were in their range, they could have red-hot shot ready
to fire at us. It was time to prepare my stratagem.

I looked over the taffrail and saw that the cutter was
towing nicely. I ordered Singh to come aboard the ship and
sent Morris down to the cutter. Morris was a gunner's
mate. He swung down into the small boat and lit the slow
match fuses in the three half barrels of black powder. The
fuses were sputtering when he threw a light boat anchor
over the side of the cutter and scrambled up to the ship. I
cut the towline and watched as the water gap between the
prize and the cutter grew. The light anchor should hold
the boat against the tide. Pulling out my watch, I went to
the binnacle where the lamp could illuminate the watch
face. As we steered toward the narrow passage, I kept a
close account of the passing minutes. I had to wait for the
gunpowder to explode before attempting to force the passage. Aloft, some of my men were sending down the
topmasts so they would not stick out above the fog bank
and give away our location as we sailed past the guns. We
were almost there; we were almost within range of the batteries. I looked at my watch again, trying to will the minute hand to move faster. Fuse is not always dependable;
the match may have stopped burning, I thought. The minute hand continued to erase time and passed the mark
where I expected the explosion. "Now!" I said aloud and
started to pray that my diversion would work. The kegs exploded. Instead of the three individual blasts I had ex-

pected, there was but one; it was loud, loud as Judgment Day, loud as if an entire powder magazine had blown up.

It must have been my imagination or a coincidental gust of wind; at the explosion, the prize surged forward as if frightened by the noise or driven by the blast. I wasn't sure if the single explosion would be as much diversion as the three I had planned, nor did I have time to consider the situation. We were in the gut between the two batteries now. I choked back an urge to start screaming as I fought fear. I wanted to live, not be killed or mutilated. If they started shooting now, particularly if they used hot shot, we would be finished. I hoped that the explosions coming from far back in the harbor would convince the French that we were deep in the bay, nowhere near the guns. They shouldn't expect the ship to reach them almost before the echo of the blasts died away.

Fear wrapped me in its chilling embrace; my tongue was numb and thick, my backbone glacial, and my lungs aching from holding my breath. My stomach felt as if a ship's rat were gnawing at its lining. The few faces I could see in the mist were grim and tight; were they as frightened as I? Would the bombardment start now? Would we all be dead or maimed in the next few seconds? The ship seemed to be picking up more speed; I looked at the sails, but the wind had not freshened. I realized then that we had been caught by the outgoing tide. Deep laden as we were, the ebb hurtled us toward the Bay of Biscay.

From the cliffs hemming us in, I could hear the sounds of men working on guns and commands shouted in French. Had they seen us, or were they still expecting a delay before a target was visible? My question was answered as a cannon went off to the starboard. The flash of fire from the cannon's muzzle lanced out through the mist.

It seemed well to our stern. I did not see or feel the ball; they had missed us by a wide margin. Other guns opened fire too, but I thought that they were just firing because another gunner had set off his cannon first. Before the guns could be traversed to point at us, we were through the gut and safe. The stratagem had worked; we were free and clear. I inhaled deeply, savoring the moist air. Let no man ever complain to me about fog in the future. Tonight the fog, the opaque, shrouding fog, had been our friend.

Chapter 7

As the prize rounded Cape Ferret and entered the open waters of the Bay of Biscay, I had her put on the starboard tack, heading north by west. Like the andante movement of a sonata, the day was breaking. The sun, slowly but majestically, rose; it was almost dead abeam of our starboard side and weakly illuminated the choppy waters of the sea. The ship moved sluggishly through those waters; it was deeply laden. I was thankful that there were no French men-of-war to pursue us, for we sailed slowly despite a favorable wind on our quarter.

There was almost enough light to see about the prize now. I sent a lookout up to the masthead to search for the *Monmouth*. She should be in sight soon. The prize was secure, the prisoners safely locked below with a guard standing over the hatch to prevent them from attempting to regain the ship. There was little I could do until we came up with Captain Gamble. I should have been allowed a second in command, a midshipman, but I had none. Wishing to leave the deck, I called for Horace Morris, the only petty officer in the cutter's crew, and told him to take charge while I went to the French captain's cabin to search for the log and manifests. "Aye aye, sir," he said as I left.

A merchant captain does not have the space of a naval captain available to him. Goods are more important than the captain's comfort; the less space allotted to him, the more paying cargo that could be carried. What should have been part of the captain's quarters was divided into cabins for passengers. The Frenchman was forced to live in two small rooms neither of which was as claustrophobic as my cubicle aboard the *Monmouth*. Despite the room, I felt closed in for the space was filled with a dense fug consisting of wine fumes, garlic, and body odor. I found the records almost immediately, but remained in the foul cabin to read them by the light of a slush lamp. The ship was the *Gloire*; she had been chartered by the French Directory to bring arms and munitions to the Spanish port of La Coruña. The French were trying to export their revolution to their neighbor. I flipped through the manifests; no wonder the *Gloire* had seemed so low in the water. She was carrying over ten thousand stand of Charleville muskets complete with bayonets and other accouterments. In addition to the guns, she carried barrels of powder and kegs of lead balls. Also listed on the manifests were a battery of 6-pounders complete with field carriages and a portable guillotine. The only thing lacking to complete an army were the men. If a lot like this were to fall into insurgent hands, *La Révolution* might spread like a malignant growth.

The stench in the cabin was more than I could abide. How the French could tolerate garlic was beyond my comprehension. Taking all the papers with me, I bolted for the door and ascended to the quarterdeck. The fresh sea air felt good. I gratefully filled my lungs, glad to be alive and successful. We had done a damn good night's work; none of my men had been killed or injured. Staying alive alone was quite an accomplishment, but returning with so rich a prize enhanced even that feat. Captain Gamble would probably be disappointed to see all of the sinners in such good health, but perhaps the value of the prize would temper his disappointment. As captain he was entitled to a full eighth of the prize money; I and my men were not so fortunate. The officers' share would be split equally among all the officers on the *Monmouth*. The same applied to the men's share. All of those who had remained safely aboard the liner would receive the same amount as those of equal rank who had risked their lives in cutting out the prize.

"Sail ho!" shouted Murphy, who was up in the foremast. "It be the *Monmouth*, sair. Wait, they's two other ships wit her, sair. I thinks the larger one be the *Renown*."

As we moved toward the distant sails, the sun rose higher and the borning day became brighter. The ships could now be seen from the quarterdeck of the *Gloire*. The *Monmouth* was hove to near a larger ship, a 74, and a third vessel, a small brig no larger than our prize, was present too. From the masts of the seventy-four-gun ship, a large blue pennant flew, a broad pennant. Either an admiral or a commodore was aboard the ship. "Morris," I said, "run up the flag and the recognition signal." I had almost told him to make our number, but this was a prize; she had no number.

The signal flags and the ensigns had been made ready; a pull on the halliards sent them squealing aloft. We were now flying the Red Ensign over the French Tricolor to show that the *Gloire* was a prize. Since the *Monmouth* belonged to the red squadron, we used the red flag. Whoever the senior officer aboard the *Renown* was, he was not a part of the channel fleet; he showed the Blue Peter. Our signals made, we watched the other ships. Flags started to erupt aboard the 74. Since I had no midshipman to read the signals, I had to do so myself. The captain of the prize was ordered to report aboard the *Renown*.

There was a small boat aboard the *Gloire;* it was about the size of a jolly boat and could be rowed by only six men. Since we had the French crew imprisoned aboard the ship, I would have hesitated taking more of my seamen off. The boat was lowered and manned. Taking the logs and manifests with me, I climbed down into the boat and took my place in the stern sheets. With so few to row, I took the tiller myself, grabbing the solid bar of wood and steering as the men worked the oars. The *Renown* knew who we were, but they challenged us as we approached. Murphy, who was pulling the lead oar, answered the hail by shouting, "*Gloire*" instead of aye aye. It was an unwarranted assertion for neither was the *Gloire* a king's ship nor was I her captain. It was a most presumptuous announcement. I could only hope that Captain Gamble would not take offense, for it was done and nothing could be done to correct Murphy's error.

We were almost to the liner now. "Toss oars," I shouted. The men lifted their oars and we glided in the last few feet, allowing the man seated on the bench next to Murphy to hook on. Clutching the records to me, I scrambled up the ropes and stepped through the entry port of the big ship. As I entered, I reached for my hat to doff it, but just then realized that I had left the hat in the cutter. Since the cutter had been blown up, I now had one less hat. Standing on the quarterdeck, alone on the weather side, were three officers. One of them was an admiral; I could tell from the twin epaulettes on each shoulder of the other two that they were captains, senior captains. I knew only one of the three, Captain Gamble. As I stood there looking at the quarterdeck, a lieutenant in a resplendent uniform detached himself from a group of officers on the lee side of the quarterdeck and walked toward me. He was obviously the flag lieutenant. "Good morning, sir," he said. "You are?"

"Lieutenant Sinjin, *Monmouth,* 64," I told him.

"I'm Willoughby, James Willoughby, flag lieutenant to Admiral Akers. The admiral would like to speak with you."

I followed Flags up the ladder to the quarterdeck and approached the admiral and the two captains. They were busy talking, so I just stood there waiting for them to acknowledge me; as I waited, I looked closely at this admiral who wished to speak with me.

Akers was in his late fifties or early sixties, I could not tell which. A tall man, as tall as I, he stooped as if he were ashamed of his height in a society of much shorter men. I knew that the stoop was not due to a nervous mannerism; it had been developed through long service on ships whose between-deck spaces were too low for a tall man to stand erect. By the time I was his age, I would have a stoop to match. His uniform was well cut by one of London's best tailors, and the gold trim, including the epaulettes, was of pure bullion. The admiral's hair was a pewter color, old pewter, and he had most of it. He did not sport a wig or louse bag, but wore his own hair clubbed in back and tied with a narrow black ribbon.

He had a large squarish head, almost too big for his body, but not quite, and an affected mannerism of cocking his head to the left when he listened. His eyes were brown, dark, dark brown and bottomless. They showed a gamut of emotion from obsidian hard to cocking spaniel soft. He seemed quite a remarkable old bird did this Admiral Akers. From just looking at him, I decided that I would rather have him on my side than in the opposition.

Gamble must have told the admiral my name, for when he finished his conversation he turned to me and greeted me with, "Welcome aboard, Lieutenant St. John. You are to be congratulated on a successful operation."

"Thank you, sir," I replied. "All credit should be given to Captain Gamble, who planned the operation." I was amazed to see Gamble flash me a grateful look. I was shocked; the man didn't seem at all sorry that I had returned. Perhaps it was the prize, I thought, but I later learned that the admiral had given him a hard time for sending only one officer on the cutting-out expedition. My words to the admiral made his position less embarrassing.

I was sure that I had pulled no wool over the admiral's eyes; he was too wise an old duck for that, but I had lessened the friction by saying what I had. I wondered too if the man realized how frightened I had been. My entire gut had seemed filled with water during the period we had been gone. I was glad that my anal sphincter had been able to hold back the flood. If this was what being a hero was like, I would prefer to be ashore and fight my battles in Parliament. Unfortunately, I neither had control of a rotten borough to elect me nor could I afford to give up my naval pay.

"Well, Admiral," said Captain Gamble, "as I told you earlier, St. John is a resolute, capable young man and very suited for command." I didn't believe my ears. Was this "Holy Bill," who thought me a blasphemer? I realized later that he had given me a good character to justify the makeup of the expedition. Gamble was speaking again, "Admiral, you told me that you needed a new commander for the *Rapid*, did you not?"

"Yes," said Akers.

"I have a senior midshipman that I can promote to acting lieutenant. That would free Lieutenant St. John, here, if you would accept him."

When thine enemy preparest a table for you, beware, I

thought unconsciously mocking the Twenty-third Psalm. Damn it, I had attended so many church services recently that whenever I was around Captain Gamble I even thought in the language of the King James translation of the Bible. I was no friend or relative of his. Why should he offer me a recommendation to be promoted? Once a lieutenant became a commander and put on that single epaulette on his left shoulder, he should be on his way to post rank. With a ship full of lieutenants, why should the admiral be looking outside for a man to promote? I didn't understand, but if I were given a chance to get away from Gamble, away from the *Monmouth*, and away from the constant threat of court-martial that hung over my head, I would grab that chance. If the admiral would have me, I was his. Not knowing what went on in Gamble's mind, I assumed his reason for recommending me was to give himself a chance once again to promote his undeserving nephew, Mr. Perkins, to acting lieutenant.

"Cap'tal idea, Gamble," said the admiral. "I would be delighted to have this young man take charge of the *Rapid* brig. Since we are sailing to Portsmouth, the prize and the *Rapid* can sail with us, for the sloop needs a refit." He turned to me, "Well, St. John, will you take the *Rapid?*"

"Thank you, sir, I will indeed."

"Done," said the admiral. "Now, Gamble, we will take the prisoners from the prize aboard the *Renown*. You will then require a smaller crew for the *Gloire*. When we get to Portsmouth, I'll detach the prize crew to Lieutenant St. John's command, for they are shorthanded aboard the sloop."

"Very good, Admiral," said Captain Gamble snuffling loudly. For a second I thought that he might be planning to pick his nose. The thought of that huge proboscis swallowing up his entire forefinger almost nauseated me. The captain had greater control than I had given him credit for; he merely rubbed the tip of his nose with the finger and said, "St. John, you have thirty-two men on the *Gloire*. You may pick ten of those to man the prize. Perhaps Captain Hale, here, can provide you with a midshipman or a master's mate to take charge of the prize crew?"

The other captain, who had been silent all the while, now spoke. "I can." At the sound of his voice, I took a closer look at him. The man, Captain Hale, looked as if he had been assembled by a cooper. His chest was a huge hogshead, his legs barrels, his arms wine pipes. All of this was topped off by a firkin with eyes, nose, and a mouth. Hale was a big man and looked tough enough to chew spikes, all the while spitting out their heads. I sensed something about him; I think it was the aroma of the fo'c'sle. I was right; I later learned that he had come up through the hawsepipe from waister to master to king's officer. Somewhere along the line he had picked up some social graces. He didn't speak often, but when he did there was nothing to show that he had been illiterate until he was past twenty.

The conversation with the senior officers now seemed at an end. I had to pick my ten from the prize crew and get my chest from the *Monmouth*. The prisoners must be made ready for the transfer. I was about to quit the quarterdeck and go about my business when Captain Gamble asked, "St. John, what happened to the cutter?"

I certainly didn't want to tell the captain that I had deliberately blown it up; I needed some excuse. "Sir, it was hit by plunging fire as we passed through the gut," I said, keeping my face straight as I lied. "We were towing it. We were lucky that the boatman was able to scramble aboard the prize before the cutter sank."

Gamble didn't seem too pleased at the news. He would

have probably preferred a higher butcher's bill, but all of us sinners had returned unharmed. The only casualty was the cutter. To balance this, he would soon be rid of me and ten more. His nephew would once again be an acting lieutenant. I turned and left the quarterdeck of the *Renown*, 74 to make preparations for taking command of His Majesty's sloop of war, *Rapid*, 14.

Chapter 8

Taking command of a ship while out to sea is a nerve-wracking experience. I didn't know what to do at first, but I couldn't let the admiral think I was in doubt. Flags made the arrangements to transfer the French prisoners to the liner. Before leaving the *Renown*, I made my list of which men to keep for the prize crew and gave it to Willoughby. The others would have to be transported back to the *Monmouth*. While the prisoners were being ferried in the launch of the *Renown*, I used the small boat from the prize to take me to the 64. I had to pick up my dunnage.

Lieutenant John Gamble had the deck when I entered through the port. "St. John," he said, "you made it back with the prize. Congratulations on your success. What happened to the cutter?"

"We lost it, sir. I'm leaving the ship; I've been given a temporary appointment to command the sloop *Rapid*, 14."

"I wish it were me," he said.

"I wish it were, sir, and I would be going along as your second. You would make a fine captain; I don't know about me. I haven't been a lieutenant long enough. I'll be a failure, I'm sure, but I'm taking the assignment just to get away from here. Thank God it's only a temporary appointment." I felt ashamed of my outburst as soon as I made it. Damn it, it was the truth; I had no more business commanding a ship than did Mr. Midshipman Perkins.

"I'm sure that you will make a fine commander, St. John," said Lieutenant Gamble. We shook hands. He was the only friend, the only real friend, I had aboard that vessel. No, there was Hallowell. He was a friend too, but a timid one. Going to the cabin for my dunnage, I ran into the third, who congratulated me on my good fortune and wished me well. I got my chest and said farewell to the *Monmouth*. As we rowed to the brig of war, I wondered what she would be like. The Royal Navy calls any vessel, be it schooner, brig, or full ship, a sloop of war if it has less than twenty guns and does not rate a post captain. When we drew near the sloop, we were hailed. "Boat ahoy!"

Murphy cupped his hands together and shouted, "*Rapid.*" This time there was justification for his act. I was the captain, the acting captain of the *Rapid*. I could see the brig clearly now. It had been hard used in a fight. Great sections of the bulwarks gleamed raw and new. We hooked on and I climbed aboard. As my head drew level with the coaming of the entry port, a bosun's pipe started to twitter. The shrill notes greeting me emphasized the difference in my status. It was only a single pipe, true, but now I was the commander of one of His Majesty's ships.

Standing near the entry port was a slim young man in a faded midshipman's uniform. He was of average height, about five feet five, and had dark hair, long hair, tied in a louse bag at the nape of his neck. His features were rather unremarkable, but nevertheless symmetrically pleasing. He seemed unmarked by life, a pleasant young man with a pleasant manner. "Actin' Leftenant Buckley, sir," he said.

"Lieutenant Sinjin," I replied.

"Welcome aboard, Captain."

Since mine was a temporary appointment, I did not have Admiralty orders to read to the crew. I did have the order from Admiral Akers; I read it to formalize the occasion. My chests had been hoisted aboard. I no longer needed the small boat, so I sent Murphy and the others back to the *Gloire*. "Mr. Buckley," I asked, "are there any other officers on board?"

"Just the master and the surgeon, sir. We lost the captain, the lieutenant, and the other midshipman when we were attacked by a French national corvette. We lost a good fourth of the crew too. Thank God the *Renown* came up when we were fighting, or we would all have been captured."

I looked around the brig, around my command, and did not like what I saw. The men mustered on the deck looked sullen and slovenly. I could understand why; pray God that I would never be in their position. They had been more than decimated; they had lost most of their officers and were about to lose the ship itself but for the fortuitous appearance of the *Renown*. Having tasted the acrid brew of defeat and failure, they were less than men. It would be up to me to restore them to dignity and confidence; I didn't think I could do it. It wasn't too important, I thought, for once we arrived in Portsmouth I would be transferred and some more experienced man given the command of the sloop.

It was no wonder the brig had suffered so badly when faced with a corvette. It was a small, frail thing, a merchant ship converted to a man-of-war, and armed so poorly that the Frenchman should have been censured for not capturing her more quickly. Before the heart was taken out of the crew they must have fought like Viking sea rovers. Seven puny 4-pounders to a side made up the armament. This was a ship of war? I almost burst out laughing. No wonder Gamble had offered my services to the admiral. This wasn't a promotion; this was a floating coffin, a tried and tested coffin.

"Would you like t' have me show you 'round the ship, sir?" asked Acting Lieutenant Buckley.

"Yes," I replied. I might as well see the worst of it now. The brig was smaller than I had first thought. It was only about one hundred sixty tons. Her normal complement was eighty-four men and six officers, but the officers included the surgeon and the master. How they managed to cram that many into such a small ship defied comprehension. Even with so many killed, the brig seemed cramped and overcrowded. If the ten men from the prize were added to the survivors, we would still be twelve men short. It did not take long to tour the ship. I was pleased to see the accommodations available to me as captain; I would have at least three times the space I had aboard the *Monmouth*, but the low deck beams would prevent me from standing in my quarters. On the way back to the quarterdeck, I stopped beside one of the cannon and plucked seven of the 3.2-inch balls from the rack. Shoving the iron spheres into my pockets, I had no difficulty in climbing the ladder. "I'm walking around with an entire broadside in my pockets," I said to Buckley. To do the man justice, he did not laugh.

The masts of the *Renown* erupted with myriad signal flags. "Preparatory, sir," said Buckley. He turned and bellowed, "Pass the word for Mr. Smythe!"

A few moments later, a man wearing the blue coat with blue lapels of the ship's master came up to the quarterdeck. He was a rotund man with the placid features common to such men. A solid bar of eyebrow, like a mustache that had been displaced upward, ran above a pair of sharp, pale blue eyes. His skin was weathered and red; great clusters of crow's-feet almost hid his sharp glance. The most striking feature was his nose, or rather the lack of one. The nose was tiny, infantile. It seemed to have forgotten to grow when the rest of Smythe had. The master introduced himself to me and then took on the task of getting the sloop under way. I pulled a telescope from its grommet over the binnacle and focused it on the prize. A midshipman stood on the quarterdeck giving orders as the *Gloire* too made ready to sail. I next turned the glass on the *Renown*. Her decks looked like a busy anthill with seamen running in all directions. It looked like chaos and confusion, but I knew that it was an orchestrated ballet. Each and every man knew where to be and how best to get there. On all three vessels, the backed foremast yards were swung, presenting their canvas to the wind. We were off. As we moved, the *Monmouth* grew smaller and smaller until only a tiny white cone of sail was visible. I was not unhappy to see "Holy Bill" and his floating church disappear; I'd be damned if I were the least bit sad.

The ship under way, I left the deck to Lieutenant Buckley and went below to my cabin. The previous captain must have been as tall or taller than I, for there was room to stretch out on his cot. I lay down, clasping my hands behind my neck, and stared up at the deck beams. A telltale compass had been let into the ceiling. From my cot I could check the direction in which the ship was sailing. I closed my eyes and thought. With a crew as small as that of the *Rapid*, it would be a major undertaking to detail as many as thirty-two men to a cutting-out party. Her launch, the largest ship's boat, would hold only sixteen. Perhaps I had done old "Holy Bill" a slight injustice in assuming that we had been sent out as a suicide mission. We had ample force to take a merchant ship the size of the *Gloire*. I thought about it longer. If Gamble were not trying to kill

me, then why had he given me a chance at glory? At last I
thought I knew the answer. Gamble was playing David the
King to my Uriah the Hittite. By exposing me in the fore
of battle, he would allow God to choose whether I should
live or die. If I lived, he would give God another chance to
change His mind. That explained much to me. If anything
happened to me on this poor excuse for a sloop, it wouldn't
be Gamble's fault; it would be God's choice. As far as I
was concerned, it was a hypocritical attitude for a man who
professed to be a good Christian, but religion often twists
men's minds in strange ways.

Although we were two officers short, Mr. Smythe was capable of keeping watch. By allowing him to do so, I was
able to take time to familiarize myself with the ship and
the crew. I wasn't too pleased with the crew, but thought
that an experienced officer should be able to restore their
confidence. I wasn't the man for the job. I shouldn't even
be a lieutenant. If the examination board members hadn't
been so overwhelmed by Pellew's reputation, I probably
would have failed the examination. Surely when we
reached Portsmouth, a competent lieutenant would be
found to take command. Possibly, I could be his first lieutenant. It would be much easier to be Jimmy One; there
would be less responsibility. But until that man was appointed, I would be in charge. If I were still captain when
the members of the prize crew joined us, I would appoint
Mr. Horace Morris gunner, for the gunner of the *Rapid*
had fallen when the captain and the lieutenant died. I
could also make Murphy my cox'n. The big Irishman was a
little rough cut for the job, but he was dependable. I
started to list the other petty officers in my mind. The
bosun, the carpenter, and the sailmaker all seemed competent enough, but the captain's clerk was barely literate. I
decided to replace him with another of the sinners from

the *Monmouth*. Samuel Goldman could cipher and write a beautiful hand. Why he, a Jew, had ever enlisted as a seaman, I didn't know. Perhaps one day I would ask him.

We had been two days at sea before I met the surgeon. Naval surgeons as a whole are a miserable lot. Men who can't make a living in civilian life gravitate to the armed services. Many of them drink to excess. When I first met Mr. Blackwell, I almost wished I had some of Captain Gamble's religious tracts on the evils of drinking. To think that my life might someday be at the mercy of this filthy, dissolute creature frightened me more than the inadequacy of the 4-pounder battery. With six rates of posted ships offering more pay to surgeons than unrated vessels like the *Rapid*, what could I expect other than the worst of a bad bargain? Life wasn't fair; I couldn't expect the finest surgeon in London to give up a lucrative practice to come aboard my ship. Mr. Blackwell made his way up to deck shortly before noon; as the man shambled his way toward the quarterdeck, I saw that he was emaciated almost to the point of starvation. He drew nearer; I could see and smell dried vomitus on his clothing, smell it even through the dense fug of rum that enveloped his person. The man was thoroughly disgusting. Angered, I looked around and saw a petty officer, Mr. Nutley, the bosun, supervising a group of seamen. "Mr. Nutley," I called. He came up toward me and stood just below the break of the quarterdeck. "Mr. Nutley, have the head pump rigged."

"Aye aye, sir," he said as he went off. The pump was soon set up. Nutley detailed two seamen to work the cradlelike pumping mechanism. I watched as they rocked it up and down and a thin stream of sea water came spurting out the hose. The doctor was still lurching around the deck; he seemed completely unaware that the sloop had received a new captain. Nutley returned to report, "Pump's rigged, sir. Wot doyer wan' me t' do wit it?"

"Mr. Nutley, take Mr. Blackwell over to the pump and hose him off, clothes and all."

The bosun looked astounded, but true to the traditions of the senior service, he knuckled his forehead and went off after muttering, "Aye aye, sir."

When the hose was turned on the surgeon, he started to scream, then collapsed on the deck. The sea water jet washed most of the filth off into the scuppers. I had sent to the galley for some hot tea. When the washing was completed, I had the sodden Blackwell brought to the quarterdeck and thrust a hot mug of tea into his shaking hand. "Drink that, Mr. Blackwell. You might say it's medicine."

He glowered at me, but raised the mug to his lips. The tea was steaming hot; he winced as he took the first sip, winced then grimaced, but he continued to drink. Finished, he put the mug down on the deck with exaggerated care, straightened up and looked at me. "Who the hell are you, Lieutenant?"

"Sinjin's the name; I'm master and commander of this sloop." I held my hand out to the wretch. He took it gravely, seemingly puzzled as to why it had been offered. "Come below, Mr. Blackwell," I said, "I wish to see if your quarters and the surgery are as foul as your person. If they are, sir, you and your mates will scrub them out. Furthermore, Mr. Blackwell, I will not tolerate a drunken surgeon. If you become inebriated again, you will be locked in the cable tier until you are sober."

I knew damn well that threats alone would not restore the man to sobriety, but what else could I do other than arrange for spirits to be kept out of his reach? Even that might prove a problem, for when alcoholics are deprived of their tipple, some go completely berserk. Possibly we could find another surgeon to replace him when we arrived in England. Until then, I would try to dry him out, but I had little confidence in my ability to do so.

The cockpit, where the midshipmen live and the surgeon performs his miracles, like the rest of the ship was tiny. It seemed too small for a surgery. When men are wounded, the surgeon removes the balls, cuts limbs, or brings the welcome peace of death; he usually does so on a surgical table made from the chests of the midshipmen. Only two of the young gentlemen were assigned to the *Rapid*. As two chests were insufficient for a table, someone had knocked together a wooden form to fill in the gap when butted against the two chests.

Cockpits are always dank, damp, and foul, but this was far worse than average. There were no midshipmen living there now; Mr. Buckley had moved to the lieutenant's cabin and the other young gentleman was dead. This left the cockpit entirely to the surgeon and his mates; they had turned it into a proper sty. Empty wine bottles had been pushed into the corners to get them out of traffic. The deck hadn't been holystoned for such a long period that it was dark gray and crusty. Such filth couldn't have accumulated in the short time since the *Rapid* fought the corvette. The previous captain must have been a slack, soft officer. I set the two loblolly boys to work on the deck, threatening to stop their rum ration if it were not white when I returned. As I went up the ladder toward the deck, I could hear the scrape of their stone prayer books against the wood of the deck. Given enough time, they would sand beneath the layer of corruption to clean wood. As I made my way back, I saw that Blackwell was not alone in his slovenly habits. The planks of the main deck needed sanding; ropes were in loose piles, lines in rat's nests instead of being coiled neatly. Even the standing rigging needed attention.

Calling for all the petty officers aboard the *Rapid*, I issued a string of orders. Although I could understand why the men had fallen into such slovenly habits, I wouldn't suffer them to continue. The ship would be cleaned up if it meant letting the cat out of the bag to bloody a few backs. The bosun started piping and the seamen fell into formation. I would inspect the men for personal cleanliness later that day when the sun became hot enough for the head pumps and a bucket brigade to wash them down. When I finished, the ship would be clean, the men would be clean, and their clothing would be clean.

Chapter 9

The sky was clear, virginal, unviolated by clouds. The wind was soft, zephyr soft; the sun, a welcome source of heat, beat on the unruffled waters. Such weather was too good to last, but while it did, I would enjoy it. The men were too busy to savor the warmth of the sun. The entire crew had been split into work parties. The rigging was being tarred down; before applying the tar, each ratline, each shroud, brace, halliard, grommet, or stay was inspected and replaced if necessary. In the tight corners men knelt on their knees and worked holystones to sand the deck. The bear worked on the more open spaces. I watched the seamen pulling the bear, that great pile of coir which had been impregnated with sand. Its action would soon get the deck white and gleaming.

Hammocks had been brought up from below, rolled and placed in the hammock nets where they would air out. Below the deck, in the men's quarters, more holystones were in use as those decks were being restored to that pristine condition so dear to the hearts of naval captains. In the galley, the cook and his mates were scouring the copper kettles with sand. After the ship was clean and the men had bathed, I would inspect for fleas and lice. If I found

any, we would have to paint them into the cracks in the
wood where they hid.

I went with the sailmaker to the sail locker to inspect the
spare suits of sail. I was aghast to find that the stored canvas showed mildew from being put away wet. More men
were called to help the sailmaker clean the sails and stretch
them out to dry properly. The carpenter showed me the
damages suffered in the encounter with the French corvette. He had done a good job of restoration. The man, a
Mr. Twombly, took pride in his work. He did not wear
that sullen look common to most of the crew. He had restored the bulwarks, jury-rigged a topmast, and reinforced
the main mast where it had been wounded by a ball. Chips
had hooped the damaged area with iron. It seemed sound
enough to hold unless we were hit by a violent storm.
When the brig reached the navy yard, they would have to
fish a new mast.

I have always believed that if men are kept busy, they do
not turn sour. Mr. Twombly was a good example; he had
been busy making repairs while many of the others lay
about feeling sorry for themselves. As long as I was in
charge of the *Rapid*, I resolved to keep the men jumping.
As soon as the ship was clean, I would exercise the great
guns, if I could dignify 4-pounders with so grandiose a title.

The next three days were uneventful. The weather was
good and with the *Renown* so close at hand, we did not
have to worry about French privateers. I kept the crew
busy from first light to dusk; they sanded, scrubbed, and
painted. They washed themselves and all their clothing,
hanging it on the rigging to dry in the mild sun. Most of
the men were co-operative; they were used to obedience; it
seemed as if most of them welcomed someone to dictate to
them and to tell them what to do. There was one exception. John Orwell, common seaman, had resisted bathing,

striking and cursing a petty officer in the process. He was to be flogged.

I'm against flogging and always have been, but in some cases no exception can be made. If Orwell escaped punishment, the rest of the crew would think me soft and slide back to their slothful ways. No, there was more than Orwell's back to consider; my authority over the men was at stake. The regulations governing a flogging are exact. The man was tried and sentenced to twelve lashes. This was announced to the entire ship. A full day must pass between sentence and execution. Orwell was locked in the cable tier and the bosun set to work making up a cat. Nutley did his job in full sight of the men. A new cat is used for each flogging. It is carefully made of rope to exact dimensions. The nine thongs are attached to a rope handle. When finished, the completed cat is put into a bag of red baize material. When used, the thongs are combed out between each stroke.

The next morning all hands were called out to witness punishment by the twittering of a bosun's pipe. The drummer stood before the formation. At a nod from me, he started a slow and solemn roll on the drumhead; the drumbeat reverberated throughout the ship. It was a melancholy sound full of evil portent. The prisoner was brought out and lashed to a grating. A heavy leather apron was strapped around his waist to protect his kidneys from the force of the cat. I waved my hand; the roll of the drum was silenced. I again read the sentence aloud to the assembled crew. "Mr. Nutley," I said to the bosun, "prepare to execute punishment."

The drummer started his roll again as the cat was let out of its baize bag. The prisoner, Orwell, was so tightly lashed to the grating that he could not move or try to twist away from the cat's claws. As he stood there waiting for the first

blow, I was reminded of a tale that had been circulating
around the fleet. It concerned an erudite but erring seaman
and a captain who hated cats. When the seaman was sentenced to be flogged, he addressed a petition to his captain
that went,

> By your honor's command
> A culprit I stand,
> An example to all the ship's crew,
> I am pinion'd and stript,
> And condemn'd to be whipt,
> And if I am flogg'd 'tis my due.

> A cat I am told,
> In abhorrence you hold,
> Your honor's aversion is mine;
> If a cat with one tale,
> Can so make your heart fail,
> O save me from one that has nine.

The sound of rope against bare flesh brought me back
from my thoughts. Unlike the poet, whose cleverness got
him off, Orwell had received the first stroke. Nine red
marks, welts, appeared on his skin; the first blow had not
drawn blood. Nutley nervously combed the tails of the cat
despite the fact that they were not bloodied. He raised his
arm and struck again. Some captains would alternate two
men to lash. By using one right-handed man and one who
was left-handed, they could spread the welts, making them
crisscross each other. With only a dozen to give, there was
no necessity for a second man even if I were given to that
sort of thinking. The drum started another roll and once
again the cat lashed out, drawing blood this time and a
scream from Orwell. A totally barbaric spectacle, I
thought, but necessary in this case. Nutley combed the
bloody lashes apart and waited for the drummer.

At last the punishment was over. Orwell, a strong man, was still conscious, but barely. The surgeon was of no use. Despite my orders, he was drunk. Orwell was treated by his shipmates, using that sovereign remedy of all seamen, salt water dipped up from the side in a leather bucket. I hoped that punishing this man would have a salutary effect on the rest of the crew. If I hadn't ordered the punishment, I would have had trouble with them. The formation was dismissed and I went below.

The isolation of a captain would have been a shocking experience to me if I hadn't been in Coventry aboard the *Monmouth*. A captain is a man apart. He has no friends aboard ship for he has no equals. Being God is a lonely role. I could talk to my officers of course, but I couldn't socialize with them. Gone was that gregarious relationship between equals, replaced by distant respect. If I had still been a midshipman, or even a lieutenant, I might have been able to find out what the crew thought of Orwell's punishment. Did they consider it fair and deserved? Did they think that it was Orwell's due? I didn't even have a cox'n who could communicate with those before the mast and pass back the information he obtained. I was only sure that after the way I worked the crew, a crew that had been allowed to relax into slothfulness, they'd all wish me well in hell. Let them think what they would; I'd be damned if I let my first command come into the yard in such slovenly condition.

The surgeon continued to present a problem. If I had been more experienced at command, I might have been able to control him. My efforts to keep the man sober were in vain. He must have had bottles of wine and rum hidden all over the ship. We kept taking them away, but he kept finding others. When at last I was exasperated enough to order him locked in the cable tier, he managed to get drunk down there. The only consolation I had was the fact that his loblolly boys had cleaned up the cockpit.

Portsmouth was in sight. We sailed, along with the *Gloire* and the *Renown*, into the roads and let the anchors run out. We had reached the end of our journey. The next few days would tell me what I was to do. Until I received orders to the contrary, I was in charge of the *Rapid*. I would see her into the yard and the repairs started.

Chapter 10

The anchorage and naval yards at Portsmouth were a busy place. From the quarterdeck of the *Rapid*, I could see most of the activity. Water hoys were pumping fresh water, powder hulks loading gunpowder, sheer rigs stepping masts, ordnance transferring cannon to ships. Ashore in the yards, sawyers bucked logs into timbers and repaired men-of-war. The sound of axes, mauls, adzes, and saws could be heard as boards were shaped to repair the damaged ships. Even the smell was unique. The tannic stench of oak sawdust and the acrid, pungent aroma of melted bitumen were swept by the land breeze out to where we were anchored. No new ships were made here, but there was enough repairing, refitting, and reconditioning going on to give work to a horde of men.

The waters of the harbor were filled with a myriad of small boats bustling to and from the ships at anchor. Bumboats brought fresh food, women, and spirits out to relieve the tedium of seamen who had not set foot on land for many months. A number of the seamen hadn't been ashore since before the current war with France. They were destined to remain afloat for fear of them running. Desertion was ever a problem, but with the ship in an English harbor, the men were near home and friends. The danger of running was even greater.

After the sloop was repaired, I would be able to replenish the barrels of salt pork and beef, the hogsheads of beer, the puncheons of rum, the kegs of lemon or lime juice, and the firkins of butter. All these were stored here ready to be issued. Why was I making plans to refit the sloop? I might not be the one in charge after the Admiralty made its decision. A hoist of flags aboard the *Renown* was noted and the message taken by Mr. Buckley, who rushed to inform me that the admiral requested my presence ashore.

I ordered my gig and was rowed to the quay. Stepping out of the boat, I told the men to wait my return. Flag Lieutenant Willoughby was waiting for me at the dock. I fell into step with him and we walked to the port admiral's quarters together. The ground felt strange and uneven beneath my feet. I was too long used to the pitching of a deck under them. To have both feet level was a strange sensation after months of walking on heeled-over decks. "I say, St. John, did anyone inform you that Admiral Akers is taking over as port admiral? That's why we were coming to Portsmouth."

I mulled Flag's statement over in my mind. It is remarkable what place coincidences can have in a person's life. If Akers had not been ordered to report to Portsmouth, then he and the *Renown* would not have been available to save the *Rapid*. If they had not taken the time to save the brig, they might not have seen and spoke the *Monmouth*. If I had not sailed the prize out just then, the admiral would have left and I would still be aboard Gamble's ship worrying about a court-martial. They call it fate, this lottery of life. I wondered if I had been lucky or unlucky when all of this happened? There was one question that I was dying to ask. Now was my chance since the flag lieutenant and I were alone. "Why me, Willoughby, why me?" He looked puzzled. "You had five lieutenants aboard the *Renown*, counting you. Why was I selected to take command of the *Rapid*?"

Willoughby laughed. "Politics, my dear fellow, politics. Your sloop is too insignificant a vessel for a lieutenant that is well connected to want. Now that we're home, the first of the *Renown* is to be posted to a frigate. The second will receive either a smaller frigate or a sloop much more powerful than your brig. The other two and I have a year's more bondage, then we too shall be posted. You, sir, were just the right man for the job."

He was right. When my uncle, Vice Admiral Bacon, died, I lost any influence I might have had. If you have an insignificant little sloop, give her to an insignificant little lieutenant; they will complement one another. I now knew why I had been picked, but I still believed that the command would go to another man, a better-connected man than I. I reckoned without taking consideration of the political position of Admiral Akers. Two days after we anchored, we were ordered to the yard for refitting. Other ships had been waiting longer, but they were forced to give over to an insignificant little brig. Within the week, the Admiralty confirmed my commission. Since the crew had been transferred to a receiving hulk where they could be kept from running while the brig was repaired, I could not read myself into command until after the ship was made ready for sea. There were errands I could attend to, or I could just take off and go to London where I would be able to sample the fleshly delights. A combination of lack of money and the desire to have the sloop as ready as possible for any eventuality kept me in Portsmouth.

The money situation resolved itself very conveniently. The Admiralty court ruled on some prizes taken by the

Arethusa over a year ago when I had been under the command of Sir Edward Pellew. I had almost two hundred guineas, golden guineas, to draw upon. It felt like a fortune. I started to think of all the things it would purchase; I needed a golden epaulette for each uniform, a new uniform, cabin stores, a wine cellar, new shoes, a decent sword —the list seemed endless and the money so limited. I managed to fight down the ebullience my new-found wealth produced and act cautiously. When I discovered the price of an epaulette made of bullion, I checked the pawnshops in hopes of finding some that had been laid up in lavender. This proved an easy feat, for many who made pledges were no longer alive to redeem them. One of the shops not only had decent epaulettes at a reasonable price, but also had a good sword that the shopkeeper was willing to sell cheaply, for it was too long and heavy for a man of average stature. Finding a good sword, one that could withstand the blow of any cutlass, crystallized the problem of the *Rapid* in my mind. The sloop was too weak and defenseless to overcome any normal warship. Merchant ships, even those who outgunned her, could be defeated by initiative and drive, but any French corvette would overwhelm the poor brig. What was needed was more fire power. A broadside of twenty-eight pounds was pathetic. Mounting larger guns would be difficult because of space limitations. An even greater obstacle to overcome would be the effect of a large charge of powder on the brig's frail timbers. I didn't know how to resolve the problem, but since Mr. Morris was to be my new gunner, I would ask him.

I went to the receiving ship and ordered Morris and Murphy to join me in the wherry boat. As we were being sculled back to the navy yard, I said, "Mr. Morris, you are to have the rate and pay of gunner. You will receive your warrant when you come aboard."

"Thank you kindly, sir."

"And you, Murphy, are to be my cox'n."

"Me muther thanks you, me fayther thanks you, and Oi thanks you, sair."

The wherry pulled up to the quay outside the ordnance depot; we disembarked. I started to explain the problem to Morris. "I'm afraid if we put short 12's or even 9's on the gun deck, the increased charge would be too much for the ship."

"Carronades, sir," he said, and then blew his nose between his fingers, flicking the mucus away. "Carronades, sir, are the answer sure as me name's Horace Morris. You only needs two pounds ten ounces of black to feed a 32-pounder. That's only a smidgeon more than the two pounds of powder we already puts into a 4-pounder."

"Capital idea, Morris. If we were to use 24-pounder carronades, we would be even closer to the two-pound service charge we now use." It did seem like a workable idea, so with the two seamen trailing me, I headed to the ordnance depot.

An extremely fat civilian clerk with a food-spattered waistcoat, a dirty stock, and an uncombed gray wig was the only one in the ordnance office. When we entered the room, he was gnawing at a drumstick. I couldn't tell if it were chicken or hare, nor did I care. He put his tidbit down and wiped his greasy fingers on the tail of his frock coat. "May I help you, sir?" he said with a sneer.

"Yes. Do you have any 24-pounder carronades in stock?"

"If you have an order, Lieutenant, I can give you a pretty pair of brass 32-pounders."

Damn, but I would have to put that epaulette on my left shoulder. I would receive more respect as commander than as a lieutenant. "I'm looking for 24's."

"Sir, you have no idea of how many people want these 32's."

I had a pretty fair idea of what the fat slob was hinting at. I pulled a golden guinea out of my fob pocket and idly tossed it in the air. "I want 24's!"

"Yes, sir, how many of them will you be needing?" he said, eyes riveted to the gold piece.

"Eighteen of them."

"Eighteen?"

"I know you have them in stock for most vessels prefer the larger carronade." The thought of parting with so many all at one time seemed to frighten the man. "I will be turning in fourteen 4-pounders," I said, "and my friend here has a brother." I slapped the gold coin on the table top, face up, and fished its twin from my pocket to place beside it. "I will get the order, then I and my friends, the two Georges, will return to see you."

"Fine, sir; I will have the carronades ready for you on your return and the receipt of the 4-pounders." He picked up his drumstick again and began to gnaw at the bone.

Admiral Akers had been removed from his Mediterranean command to receive a political plum. He was now the port admiral here at Portsmouth. In this new position, he would probably become a very rich man before he was transferred. A port admiral receives a portion of all prizes captured by ships operating under his orders. Akers had been friendly enough until now. I hoped to persuade him to authorize the changes I wished to make in the *Rapid*. We walked from the ordnance office to Akers office. Leaving the two seamen to wait for me outside, I opened the door and entered the anteroom.

I was in luck. I only had to warm my backside against a chair bottom for ten minutes before the admiral had me ushered into his room. "Ah-hah there, Lieutenant St. John. What brings you here this morning?"

"Sir," I said, "I wish to make a change in the armament of the sloop *Rapid*."

"Very good, St. John; tell me more about your plans."

"Sir, I would like to replace the broadside 4-pounders with eighteen 24-pounder carronades and put a short 9 in for a bow chaser."

"You'd be giving up distance, St. John."

"Sir, with 4-pounders and a broadside of twenty-eight pounds, I would be giving up nothing compared to what I gain. How far is the shot of a 4-pounder effective?"

"Haahmmm, yes, of course, I dare say you're right. There have been all carronade ships before, but they are larger. They had to give up long-range effectiveness for metal. But in your case, you have neither long- nor short-range effectiveness. Approved, sir."

"Thank you, Admiral. When may I pick up the authorization?"

"Tomorrow, St. John."

"Thank you, sir."

Chapter 11

It was a typical June day in England. Sea mist hung heavy over the harbor, presenting an almost impenetrable wall and hiding the ships at anchor. The sky gloomed dark overhead while the sun was conspicuous by its absence. Aboard His Majesty's sloop of war *Rapid*, my mood did not match the weather. My spirits were ebullient. The repairs to the brig had been finished; as soon as all the stores were loaded, we would be ready for sea. The 24-pounder carronades gleamed brightly despite the lack of sun; their fresh black paint was deep and lustrous. We were no longer a sitting duck for any French vessel. Instead of a meager twenty-eight-pound broadside, we could now throw two hundred sixteen pounds of metal, more iron than a 12-pounder frigate. I looked at the two guns per side that had been emplaced on the quarterdeck and wished that I could have placed others on the fo'c'sle too, but that would have raised the number of guns to twenty and made the *Rapid* a post ship to be commanded by a captain.

As I stood there, feeling proud of my new command, a powder hulk signaled us that it was ready to come alongside. I ordered the galley fire put out and the coals dumped; when black powder is loaded aboard a ship, all fires, candles, pipes, and cigars must be extinguished to prevent an explosion. When the fires were all doused, we signaled to the hulk, which warped itself to us and started to off-load barrels of powder.

The powder was all below, safely stowed in the magazine by Horace Morris, the gunner. Before we could light the galley fire, it was necessary to clean up any spilled powder. Black powder is dangerous stuff; it can be ignited by stepping on it with a shoe. "Rig the head pump," I ordered. The decks were wet down and mopped clean by the barefooted seamen.

The powder hulk gone, a water hoy approached, shrouded in tendrils of mist. Soon they would be pumping fresh water aboard to fill the casks newly scoured and checked by the cooper. We had already received nets full of 24-pounder balls, quarter kegs of lemon juice, firkins of butter, hogsheads of beer, English beer, bags of ship's bread, barrels of flour, lard, salt pork, and salt beef. What vegetables I had been able to pry loose were aboard too.

The crew had seemed glad to be taken off the receiving ship and transferred back to their familiar quarters. They still seemed a sullen lot, but the sight of the refitted sloop did cheer them slightly. It had been hard on them to be cooped up aboard a hulk anchored only a few hundred yards from England and home. If given a chance, many of them would have deserted; even back on the *Rapid,* I could not trust them. I did have the ten from the *Monmouth* that would probably be loyal; after all, they had prize money coming and had served with me before. Thinking of desertion, I shuddered and tried to put it out of my mind. I was only glad that no one had tried; we were shorthanded enough already. If any of them had tried to run and was caught, the punishment would have been severe. I shuddered again at the thought of having one of my men whipped through the fleet. With so many ships here, it would be a death sentence.

I had been aboard the brig when the crew was returned. They were marched to the quay in a long line under marine guard. They might just as well have been prisoners, these Britons, these free men; all those who entered service were no better than bound servants or slaves despite the noble words of "Heart of Oak." I watched them closely as they climbed aboard ship after being ferried from the shore. I was looking for a sign, any sign of interest or alertness. Some of the men reacted as I had hoped to the repairs and the new armament; others did not seem to notice that any change had been made. I marked down the names of the alert men for future promotion.

As I watched, one seaman, James Fry by name, walked over to one of the new carronades. He stood there staring at it, as if it were some strange creature, then started to pat it on the flank as if it were a horse. As he patted, he spoke to the gun in the soothing voice a stable hand uses to a recalcitrant mare. "Us'll fix they Frenchies, lass; us'll do it, jes you wait und zee." He then reached to the rack and almost reverently picked up one of the six-inch, twenty-four-pound balls; he examined it closely, then shrugged and put the black-painted iron ball back in the rack with its brothers.

Just then Horace Morris came aboard. He and Murphy were not in the lot from the receiving hulk. I saw him and called, "Mr. Morris, if you have a moment, please come here." Although expressed in such a way as to give him an alternative, any suggestion from a captain is in reality an order. Mr. Morris had nothing more pressing, nor did I expect otherwise. He came to me immediately. "Morris, please nip below to my cabin and fetch the duty roster book."

"Aye aye, sir," he said as he dashed below.

When Morris returned and handed me the book, I looked up James Fry. He was a waister, a man of no particular talent other than to do as he was told. The man looked rather stupid, but his actions impressed me favorably; I liked the way he had behaved with the gun. "Mr. Morris, there is a waister, Fry by name, who might work out as your assistant. I want you to work with him for a while. If he turns out satisfactory, we will rate him gunner's mate." Morris left and immediately sought out Fry. From where I stood, elevated on the quarterdeck, I could see them talking together. Short, bald, wiry Morris; tall, fat, sloppy Fry; they made a disparate pair.

Mr. Buckley, during the time repairs were made to the gun brig, had taken and passed his examination for lieutenant; he had been assigned back to the *Rapid*. He seemed good material to me and now that the Admiralty had seen fit to promote him, he should work out very well. No new officers had arrived yet, but I had Admiral Akers' assurance that two midshipmen and a surgeon were assigned to the ship. Mr. Blackwell, the former surgeon, had headed straight for the nearest tavern when we allowed him on shore. He had drunk himself almost senseless, then on leaving the inn had started to walk along the quay; he fell in and drowned. This was unfortunate for Mr. Blackwell, but most convenient for me. I did not have to file formal charges against him.

With all the men aboard, it was time to read myself into command. I passed the word for Mr. Buckley and had him assemble all hands. I lifted the flap of the canvas envelope holding my orders and pulled out the papers. I then read them aloud, savoring each and every word.

"By the Commissioners for Executing the Office of Lord High Admiral of the United Kingdom and Ireland . . . to Lieutenant John St. John . . . His Majesty's gun brig *Rapid* willing and requiring you forthwith to go on board and take upon you charge and command as master and commander in her accordingly."

It was done. I was now the captain of the *Rapid*. From this minute on, I controlled the lives and destinies of the entire crew. Buckley dismissed the men; they went back to their duties. He and I remained on the weather side of the quarterdeck, talking. It was now my weather side whenever I chose. From the fighting top, the lookout hailed a small boat that was approaching us. "Aye aye," the boatman cried back in answer. The wherry contained an officer; it could be either of the midshipmen or the surgeon. The newcomer climbed up through the entry port and faced the quarterdeck. He almost stumbled as he came through the port. He was a tall, painfully skinny young fellow in a poorly tailored midshipman's uniform. He wore the gloomiest look about him I have ever seen on any individual not on his death bed, but his eyes belied his mournful, long face. They were bright, beady, merry, and actively darting around the ship to evaluate the vessel and the men. There was a certain undefined look in those eyes that I tried to place; bold, perhaps; rebellious, probably; intelligent, certainly. I tried, but had no success; he was an enigma. The somber look of the midshipman went well with his swarthy complexion. Looking at the youngster closer, I saw that part of the darkness was the faint stubble of a blue-black beard. He was closely shaven, but the blue color persisted nonetheless.

"Sir, Midshipman Hector H. Hornswoggler reporting, sir."

It was an outrageous name, a most improbable name; it

was monstrous, heinous, and atrocious: it was a flagrant insult to my intelligence, an indecent practical joke. The enormity startled me, dumbfounded me; I could not speak. I stared at him, saying nothing. Although well bearded, the new midshipman was still a boy, about seventeen years of age. At last I found my tongue. "Welcome aboard, Mr. Hornswoggler," I said, and then because my curiosity was great, I added, "What does the middle initial stand for?"

"Hannibal, sir."

That was entirely too much. I was incensed at him for trying to spoof his captain. "Mr. Hornswoggler, sir, do you have your commission with you?"

He handed me the paper. There it was in black and white, finely written in a copper-plate script: Hector Hannibal Hornswoggler, Midshipman. I handed the papers back to him. He smirked, a superior smirk, an almost supercilious smirk, but said nothing as he put them away. It was true. Lord, what a name to be cursed with. A name like that could warp a man's personality. It did have one compensation; if ever he performed some heroic feat, on hearing about it no one would say which Hornswoggler. As a name it was distinctive. Possibly it would be a worse curse to be named John Smith.

I turned Mr. Hornswoggler over to the tender care of our bosun, Mr. Nutley, who was to take the young gentleman and his chest below to the cockpit where the midshipmen are berthed. The sea chest was swayed aboard near the waist of the ship. From the quarterdeck, I had no difficulty in hearing the bosun's comments when he saw the chest; they would have been audible on the orlop deck or from the masthead. "What blue-nosed, blue-bollocked son of a buttock's broker sold ye that fer a sea chest! It's too big, sir. A man could live in that bleedin' chest—lookee 'ere, sir, you got 'most as much room in that chest as the

leftenant 'as in 'is cabin." Nutley fixed the midshipman
with a stern gaze. Since Hornswoggler was over six feet tall
and the bosun only five four, this was quite an accomplishment. "Chips!" shouted Mr. Nutley, "pass the word
for Chips." The carpenter came on the run when his fellow
petty officer called. Soon I heard the rasp of a saw against
wood. The bosun had made Chips saw the sea chest in
two, just aft of the keyhole. As the carpenter, Hornswoggler, and the sawed-apart chest made their way below,
I could hear Nutley saying, "Daft chest makers! Y'ud
think they could put the bloody lock on the end of the
bleedin' chest. . . ."

I gave young Hornswoggler no further thought, for another boat was approaching the ship. This wherry contained two officers intended for the ship. They were our
new surgeon, Mr. Thomas Yates, and the other midshipman, Mr. George Dinsdale. They climbed aboard and paid
their respects to the quarterdeck. Mr. Dinsdale was the an-
tithesis of Mr. Hornswoggler, being fair where the other
was dark, short where he was tall, with a cheerful-looking,
snub-nosed, freckled face, where Hornswoggler's was
gloomy. Dinsdale was much younger; he looked about thir-
teen. He also looked frightened. "Mr. Dinsdale," I said,
thinking to ask him some innocuous question to put him
at ease.

"Sir," he answered, broke wind loudly, and started to
cry. He was young, but it seemed most unseemly for an
officer of the king to be in tears. I wondered for a second
what had frightened him, then realized that it was me. The
captain of a king's ship can be a frightening figure to those
under him.

"Dismissed, Mr. Dinsdale," I said, and turned to talk to
Mr. Yates. I hoped that the new surgeon would turn out to
be of a more sober disposition than the previous one.

While Mr. Dinsdale was being taken to the cockpit by one of the seamen, I had Mr. Yates accompany me to my cabin. I wanted to size up the man. He seemed to be an improvement on the late Mr. Blackwell, at least he appeared clean and neat and did not smell like the inside of a rum barrel. The *Rapid* was no proper man-of-war; we had no marines aboard. I did not have the luxury of a sentry to guard my cabin door. I opened the door and crouched to enter. Still crouching, I made for my table in a sort of squat walk and deposited my rear in the chair. There was ample room in the cabin for me to sit up straight. The surgeon, who stood only five feet five, followed me into my quarters walking almost upright. I motioned him to a chair and reached for a bottle of port. As Yates seated himself, I poured a modest tipple for myself, then handed him the bottle and a glass. To my astonishment, the man refused the wine. Yates was a Welshman, an argumentative people, but one that had been very receptive to Methodism. When it comes to religion, I feel that every man has a right to his own opinion so long as he doesn't try to force it upon others. I'm even willing to accept Catholics and Jews, if they will do their job properly. Gamble had left a rather sour taste for Methodists in my mouth, but if Yates didn't try to force literature on the crew, his choice of religious dogma wouldn't bother me. Since the man didn't drink, I wondered about his reason for joining the Navy. It could be that he was an incompetent butcher or a runaway from debt as I had been just a few years back. He might be fleeing from a woman and matrimony. I would ask him neither his reason for joining the Navy nor his religion. Suffice it to say that he was clean and sober. Time would tell if he were competent in his professional duties.

The ship was restored to seaworthiness; the supplies were laden; the entire crew was aboard. We were ready to put to

sea, but could not do so until we had orders. Now that the
last officer had joined the brig, it was time for me to report
to the port admiral. It would be best to change my clothing, I thought. Rubbing my hand along my face, I decided
that I needed a shave too. I called for a basin of hot water
and went below to my cabin. Grabbing my toilet roll, I
opened it and removed a razor, mirror, soap, and a brush.
The skylight of the day cabin opened onto the quarterdeck.
I pushed it up, opening it with my hand, and stood erect;
my head projected through the hole above the quarterdeck
planking. Murphy brought the basin of hot water and
placed it next to my head. Propping up my small, polished
steel mirror on the deck in front of me, I opened my
Wilkinson razor and got ready to shave. I was in the habit
of looking at my face in the shaving mirror at least every
other day. In all the years I have done so, I had never
found my visage frightening, intimidating, or cruel. My
nose had been broken and was no longer straight, but that
should not have made me appear sinister. Of course the
cutlass scar on my left cheek, which I received when we
boarded the *Cléopâtre*, ran from the periphery of my jawbone to my forehead, but it did not alter the classic sym-
metry of my features. I didn't consider it a mean face; in
fact, I thought I was rather handsome compared to many—
an opinion seemingly shared by some young ladies. Regardless of my opinion, Mr. Midshipman Dinsdale had been
terrified by my appearance.

I finished my shave, removed the tools from the deck,
ducked my head back into the cabin, and closed the
skylight. The brig was too small to bother with a captain's
servant or a private cook. I dressed myself in a fresh uniform, my good one, and prepared to leave the ship. The
epaulette on my left shoulder felt strange and heavy, but it
did impart a certain sartorial splendor to my uniform.

As I came up on deck, my gig was being swayed into the water. Many captains decorate their gigs or have them specially painted in distinctive colors. I had followed this example not only with the gig, but also with all of the other boats on the *Rapid*. Instead of a blue and white gig, or an all white gig, mine was painted black, dull, dead black. My oarsmen wore white trousers with black shirts. It was a rather funereal effect, heightened by the oars, which were painted black too. My choice of color was deliberate; I did not choose it because I was of a morbid or melancholic disposition, nor did I select black just to be different. My reason was more pragmatic. A black boat sent on a cutting-out party would be less visible at night. Black oars would not flash white in the moonlight.

Taking my place in the stern sheets at the tiller, I ordered the boat to the quay. The jet oars rising in perfect unison still gave the small boat the look of a bird skimming over the waters, but the look was that of a rook, not a gull. We rowed to the quay nearest the port admiral's office. A lounger, an old seaman by the look of him, was seated on a piling despite the cold, overcast weather. As I called, "In oars," and we glided up to hook on, he spat tobacco into the water.

"That's quite a funeral barge ye've got there, Capting," he called in a derisive voice. I did not deign to answer, but Murphy's face seemed to be approaching the red of his hair.

"Ignore him, Murphy," I said. "Wait here; I hope to return shortly."

"Aye aye, sir," replied the Irishman, reaching into his pocket for his plug. He worried off a large chew and started to work his jaws in a rhythmic manner. From the speed he was chewing the tobacco, I knew that he was more than a little upset at the lounger's remarks.

Admiral Akers was not in his office, but his flag lieuten-
ant was. Flags handed me a sealed envelope, saying,
"We've been expecting you, St. John. Here are your orders.
You may open them when you get aboard your vessel."

"Thank you, Willoughby," I said, and then left, holding
the canvas envelope in my hand. I could feel the lead shot
enclosed with the orders. It seemed ridiculous to have
packed it that way, since I was to open it once I was aboard
the *Rapid*, but the bureaucratic mind works in strange and
wonderful ways. If I were to be captured by the French
while at anchor in Portsmouth Harbor, I would be able to
drop my orders over the side, secure in the knowledge that
they would sink to the bottom.

The gig was standing off from the quay by about twenty
yards. Good man Murphy—if one of the gig's crew wished
to run, he would have had to swim for it. The average British Jack couldn't swim twenty feet much less twenty yards.
I signaled for them to come up to the wharf and watched
as the black oars dipped into the water. I was almost surprised that the gig did not utter a raucous caw, caw as it
headed toward me. I relieved Murphy at the tiller and we
headed back for the brig. The canvas envelope and the
unopened orders preyed on my mind. What new dangers
would I be facing? I almost envied Willoughby, but I
could never take his place. It requires a special person to be
a flag lieutenant. I would rather face death than take his
job.

Once aboard the *Rapid*, I went to the privacy of my
cabin and slit the wax seals on the canvas envelope. After
the usual verbiage regarding the Admiralty, my message
was succinct. I was to take the brig out and harass French
merchant shipping. It was a license to steal—to engage in
lawful piracy. A tiny sloop of war is incapable of fighting in

the battle line; its only function is to carry messages, scout, or capture enemy merchant men.

Even before changing the armament, the *Rapid* was capable of destroying commerce. Acting directly under the port admiral, my orders gave me the license to go where I would and do unto the enemy wherever I might find him.

Chapter 12

The Admiralty giveth and the Admiralty taketh away; blessed be the name of the Admiralty. I had just received the orders dreamed of, lusted for, prayed for, and desired by every man who ever commanded a ship. It was an independent command. For the next twelve weeks, I was my own master, answerable to no man. It was my chance at prize money. Instead of this potential cornucopia, I could have received an assignment to escort a convoy of merchant ships, or have been put to work transporting orders to some far-off portion of the globe. I was ecstatic, delighted, gratified, and pleased with the orders. They made me feel so exuberantly happy that I wished to climb the shrouds and shout the news from the masthead; I didn't. It would have been damaging to my new position of respectability. I was now a commander and beyond such boyish enthusiasms.

I sat at my table and reread the orders. Prize money, that chimerical lure, pieces of eight, I thought, but then realized that we were not at war with Spain. All prize money would have to come from the land of *Liberté, Égalité, et Fraternité*; in other words, from the land of the frogeaters. French commerce had been driven from the seas, making prizes harder to find than they had been at the beginning of the war, but there were still prizes to be found. The coasting traffic had not been stopped and, if anything, the hordes of privateers had increased. Much of France's boat traffic moved in internal canals, but canals and rivers could never completely replace sea routes. To transport the cargo of a ship, even one as small as the *Rapid* would take a long line of wagons and drivers, a line well over a mile in length. Unless the teams were replaced or rested there was a limit to how far they could pull a dray. Even wagon drivers need rest. If a wagon train moved a load as far as twenty miles in one day, it was most efficient. The roads were another problem; they were bogs during the rainy season, dusty during the dry summer, and impassible when it snowed. France had neither the wagons, the teams, nor the drivers to take all traffic off the sea. If she were forced to try, the cost would bankrupt her already shaky government, while the number of men, mules, oxen, and horses would drain the armed services. So long as England made the passage of goods by sea difficult, France would suffer.

I put the orders back into their envelope and placed them in the top drawer of my desk. Locking the drawer with a key, I left the cabin to go on deck. Lieutenant Buckley was pacing up and down on the quarterdeck, holding an earnest conversation with Mr. Hornswoggler. When they saw me approaching, they moved over to the lee side but continued their talk. I interrupted them with, "Mr. Buckley, prepare to get under way."

"Mr. Hornswoggler," said Buckley, "pass the word for Mr. Smythe." As the midshipman left, Buckley picked up a tin speaking trumpet and bellowed, "All hands, all hands, prepare to hoist anchor."

Men came boiling up the companionways and onto the deck. Their bare feet slapping against the sanded oak planks of the deck produced a curious drumming sound, loud but not unpleasant. The *Rapid* had a small, single-headed capstan up on the main deck. Thank God we had it rather than a windlass, for its action was much quicker. Fitting the eight-foot-long capstan bars into the square slots in the head, four men got on each of the four bars and started to walk the anchor off the floor of the anchorage. We could raise it with so few men because our anchor was much lighter than that of a sixty-four-gun ship like the *Monmouth*, almost two tons less.

The muscles of the sixteen men overcame the inertia of the half-ton anchor. As they went around, the metal pawls of the capstan clicked with each increment the anchor was raised. Slowly at first and then more rapidly, sounding almost like a pair of Spanish castanets, the pawls played their tune. "Hove short!" cried a lookout from the bow; the music of the pawls stopped. The anchor was now straight up and down, still holding the ship in position. It would now be possible to make sail. The topmen were in the masts ready for the command. "Sheet home!" shouted Mr. Buckley, his voice magnified by the shiny, black trumpet. The sails were let fall into place and clewed there. As the topmen slid down to the deck, the waisters manned the braces and perfected the set of the yards. The foremast sails were backed, allowing the wind acting on one mast to offset that acting on the other. "Hoist the anchor!" shouted Buckley. The big anchor was pulled the rest of the way up, up out of the water, up to the bow of the ship where it was catted home, ready to be dropped if needed. The brig, even though the anchor was out of the water, was held in place by the action of the wind as if it were still anchored. On Buckley's command, the waisters hauled the foreyards partly around, presenting the sail to the wind. The *Rapid* heeled, swinging like a monkey-tailed swivel, and faced the harbor entrance. The foresails were pulled the rest

of the way at the command, "Lay her before the wind!"
The ship began to move out of the harbor.

When the Isle of Wight became visible to our starboard,
I knew we were in the Channel. We were off to war, but
this time I was in charge of the destiny of every man
aboard the ship. It was an awesome feeling, eerie, uncanny,
and strange; it felt as if I were playing God. I had faced the
enemy before and each time I had done so it was with
great trepidation. I knew that disease kills more sailors
than gunfire, but facing the broadside of an enemy can still
curdle the guts despite that knowledge. Up till now, the
captain would engage or not as he saw fit. Mine had not
been to wonder why, only to do my assigned job. If I were
in command of a battery, it was, "Load, you sons of
bitches, load! Swab out, damn it, swab out—dip those
woolly-headed bastards in the water and swab out! Train
your guns, heave, damn it, heave, you back door gentlemen, heave. Swab, load, heave, train, prime, FIRE!!!!!!"
My only responsibility was to my section of guns. Up
above, on the quarterdeck, the open quarterdeck, the captain walked, paced, or stood, despite sniper fire from the
enemy tops, despite grape and canister. He walked in plain
sight, marked by his golden epaulettes, and still directed
the fight. His were all decisions, his the strategy, his the responsibility. I was only a cog to his wheel. Until today, I
had never wondered about the fears and the abilities of the
other men on board. Now as much as they would be dependent on me, I would be dependent on them. Without
cogs, the wheel does not move. This crew was not untried,
but they had been engaged in a near disastrous fight; they
were sullen and unco-operative. Most of their officers had
been killed in that fight. Would these men now face battle
bravely regardless of their inner fears, or would they panic?
Did they respect my abilities enough to fight even if they

were afraid? How could they? My abilities, if any, had never been demonstrated. My lieutenant was better known to them than I. He had been aboard when the previous captain had been killed. Only the chance arrival of a British 74 had saved them from capture or death. How would this man react under fire? I had two new midshipmen; they were even more of an enigma. They had never been to sea before, but one of them burst into tears at the sight of my kindly face. A fine way for a king's officer to behave. As I nervously paced back and forth, I wondered if this new command would be more than I could handle.

Since I had received no instructions about where to cruise, I had decided to head directly for the French coast. If I traveled as the sea gull flies, across from Portsmouth is the Bay of the Seine, the mouth of the river that leads to Paris. Once there, by going north, I could sail toward Calais or by turning south, around the Cherbourg Peninsula, sail past the Channel Islands. Jersey, Guernsey, Sark, and Aldernez were in British hands despite their proximity to France. At any of these, I would be able to stop and pick up fresh food and water. The French coast was an attractive place to look for prizes; innumerable bays and inlets along the shore provided places of refuge for a coaster. Most of the coasting traffic moved at night. It was more dangerous to sail after the sun went down, but in the dark there was a greater chance for the French ships to avoid the Royal Navy.

About twenty miles out of Portsmouth, we found ourselves alone at sea. How long that would last, I did not know, for the Channel receives much traffic. Many of the ships belonged to either Britain or to neutral nations. As long as we were free of this congestion, it would be a good time to exercise the guns. Battle stations are an all-hands situation: no one is spared from duty. Even the captain's clerk is expected to fight. Goldman was an experienced gun captain. Following my policy of putting the tested men who had come over from the *Monmouth* with me into positions of responsibility, I had appointed the clerk as a quarter gunner, in charge of a section of guns.

At my order to exercise the guns, Mr. Nutley started to trill away at his bosun's pipe. All hands rushed to their positions. We did not take down the partitions, but we did douse the galley fire to allow the firing of a practice round. Horace Morris, the new gunner, went below to pass out powder cartridges and priming quills. Each carronade crew gathered around their weapon. "Unlash your guns!" I shouted.

The breechings were flung off, the carriages pulled back, and the men went through the motions of loading, traversing, elevating, and firing. At the command, "Fire!" they simulated releasing the flintlock and then they pretended to swab out and reload. The short carronades would load faster than cannon; with their screw-operated elevation device and wheeled traverse, they would be easier to line up on a target. Carronades used smaller gun crews. Even with a dozen men short, we could man all of the guns on both broadsides. With a little practice, we should be able to equal or exceed the three shots every six minutes achieved by well-trained English gun crews. From my own experience, I knew that most French crews could serve their guns only half as fast as this. The drill was most realistic. Sand had been sprinkled on the decks to prevent slipping. Tubs of salt water to cool the gun and wet the swabber's mop were put into position next to each gun. We had even lighted the slow match to fire the guns if the flintlock failed. After four rounds of dry fire, I thought it time to use powder and ball.

I ordered a wooden cask tipped off into the sea as a target for the guns. Mr. Morris sent the powder monkeys up with cartridges of black powder. They looked tiny compared to the charge of a 24-pounder long gun, but the iron balls that followed the powder and wadding down the muzzles of the gun were the same six-inch balls we had used on the main gun deck of the *Monmouth*. Any ship receiving our broadside would be devastated when those heavy balls hit her, smashing through bulwarks. The cask was bobbing up and down in the water. It made a difficult target.

All the guns were loaded, ready to fire. "Number-one gun, fire at will!" At Buckley's command, the gun was pointed, fired, and swabbed out. They had missed the cask. One after the other, the gun crews took their shot at the target. The sound of the carronades was surprising; their short length increased the muzzle blast, making them sound as loud as if not louder than long guns of the same caliber. Eventually, the cask was hit; most of the shots had struck near enough to the small, bobbing object to satisfy me. Although the guns had been swabbed out, they were not reloaded. I only wanted one round with live ammunition.

As the guns went off, I looked at the men. Buckley, a scarf bound around his ears to soften the explosion sound, seemed in his element. His eyes gleamed and he strode up and down behind the guns with an arrogant swagger as he urged each gun pointer to take careful aim. Hornswoggler, who was assisting Buckley today, looked even gloomier than ever, but as I watched he seemed to be dancing a tiny jig behind one gun crew. Their gun went off at that moment; the air was filled with chicken feathers and smoke, for that gun was on the lee side of the ship; the wind had blown the feathers inboard onto the ship. I looked at Hornswoggler, thinking I had detected a wicked gleam in his eye, but if I had, it was quickly gone. His somber face was completely free of guilt. If I had not seen the little dance he had performed in anticipation of the gun going off, I never would have suspected him of packing the feathers into the wadding. The boy was a practical joker. Knowing this, I wouldn't let him gull me. "Mr. Hornswoggler," I shouted, "you and the crew of number-six carronade will clean up the deck. I don't want to see any feathers when you finish."

"Aye aye, sir," the young scoundrel said with a straight face.

The practice firing continued. Mr. Dinsdale, who was on the quarterdeck as signal midshipman, seemed rather unsure of himself. He was the youngest officer on the *Rapid*. Not yet fourteen, Dinsdale should have been in the nursery, not out here trying to command men, not out here where he could be killed in battle or die from disease. England has long had immature officers with tiny, piping voices. The seamen seem to go out of their way to help the youngsters mature. As each carronade went off with a loud, plank-shuddering blast, Dinsdale shivered and appeared frightened. After the reverberations died away, he smiled and was fine until the next gun went off.

The "great gonnes," carronades in our case, having been exercised, I had the crews replace the breechings and secure them in place. Ordering Chips to inspect the gun mounts for possible damage, I returned to my cabin, leaving the deck to Mr. Buckley. The carpenter finished his inspection and reported back to me. No damage had been done to the timbers of the ship. They stood up as well to the recoil of the carronades as they had to the 4-pounders once installed. Everything was in order. I thanked the man and watched him leave. We would be nearing the French coast in a few hours. It would be wise to take a nap until then. If a sail were sighted, I would be notified. I removed my shoes and coat, but left my other clothing on. I stretched out on the cot; for a few seconds I listened to the timbers of the ship groan as she worked in the sea, then oblivion.

Chapter 13

I woke from my nap at the sound of knuckles against my cabin door. It was close in the room, almost as close as the tiny cubicle I had occupied aboard the *Monmouth*. I should have propped the skylight open for fresh air before I took my nap. The rapping sounded again. "Come," I called.

It was Murphy. "Land's been sighted, sair."

"Very good, Murphy. I'll be right up on deck."

The land mass in view was the Pointe de Barfleur on French maps and Barfleur Point on English ones. It projected out into the Channel looking much like a miniature Spain turned the wrong direction on the charts. Barfleur Point separates the Bay of the Seine from the Gulf of St. Malo and the Channel Islands. We had made a slow passage; dusk was falling and the large land mass looked like a low rain cloud far off on the horizon. There was still light enough to round the point and sail toward Caen along the hoop of the bay. Long before we reached the mouth of the River Seine, it would be dark. To avoid capture by British ships, coasting vessels would move after night fell. I hoped to be in their path when they made their move.

"Mr. Buckley," I called, "I want two lookouts to each mast; you will change them every hour." Fresh eyes aloft might spot the movement of an enemy vessel even on a dark night. We paralleled the shore, moving slowly. Everyone aboard was alert, but we saw nothing. The gloom of dusk deepened into the Stygian blackness of a night unrelieved by the moon. This would not continue long, for the moon, a gibbous moon, was scheduled to rise soon. On time, the double convex, humpbacked moon took its place in the firmament and cast its wan glow on the sea and on the *Rapid*. I was standing on the quarterdeck with Lieutenant Buckley. In the pale light of Diana, I could see that his jaw was tightly clenched making large, protuberant knots at the angles. His face was pale and appeared moist. His eyes blinked rapidly, very rapidly. I was alarmed at his appearance; he seemed unwell. "Are you all right, Mr. Buckley?" I asked.

He looked at me, or rather right through me. It was as if I weren't there. I passed my hand before his eyes, but he did not see the motion. It was as if he were in a trance or sleepwalking. Suddenly he started to scream, "Haul down the flag! We surrender! For God's sake, cease fire!" He collapsed onto the deck and started sobbing, harsh sobs that wracked his entire body. Buckley was back on the *Rapid* when she fought the corvette. He was reliving that episode. The ordeal then had been too much for him. I looked around; if any crew members had heard him, they were ignoring his fit. It seemed impossible that his voice had not been heard. The news would be all over the ship in the morning. I would have to speak with Buckley, but I doubted that it would do much good. I started to feel sorry for myself; the crew was sullen, the first lieutenant mad, one midshipman a practical joker while the other was a puking, mewling babe in arms. Buckley seemed over his crying jag; I sent him below, taking his watch myself.

The hours sped by as we continued to cruise north along

the French coast. Time was marked by the sound of the ship's bell every half hour. As we saw the mouth of the River Orne, directly abeam, I heard the lookout hail the deck. "Sail ho! Two points offa starboard bow."

"Beat to quarters!" I shouted.

The *Rapid* had only one drum and no fifes; since we had no marines, we had no marine drummer. The job of beating the drum to call the seamen to their stations fell to one of the nippers. When the anchor was hoisted, the lad's job was to nip the anchor cable to the endless rope messenger and guide it to the cable tier. If we had a marine drummer, his job during battle would be that of powder monkey, fetching cartridges from the magazine to the guns. The lad started to roll his sticks on the tightly stretched head of his calfskin fiddle. The sound, a martial sound, penetrated every corner of the sloop. The boy's stickwork was erratic, his rhythm sporadic, but I thought that I could make out the beat of "Heart of Oak." Despite the fact that I have heard better drumwork, the message was clear and received by all members of the crew, who rushed to their action stations. Buckley was on the main deck, ordering the crew to load the broadside carronades. He sounded calm; I hoped for the best. Young Hornswoggler was at his regular station, the quarterdeck carronades, instead of the main deck. I resolved to keep an eye on the young man. There is no place for practical jokes during a battle. In fact, I didn't hold with them at any time or place, but until I could devise a way to teach the young scalawag that mischief doesn't pay, I would say nothing, but watch him carefully. A reprimand would not do much good, I knew; I wanted some spectacular way to drive the lesson home.

The *Rapid* was living up to her name; the brig was catching up with whatever the lookout had sighted, for a tiny triangle of canvas was now visible from the quarterdeck despite the muted glow of the moon. I looked at the sky; the moon was much higher now. The change in the angle allowed even a gibbous moon to illuminate the night. I looked out at the outline of the shore; we had placed ourselves, like a stopper, in the mouth of the river and were blocking the entrance. There was no longer a chance for the coaster to scuttle to safety so long as we blocked off the Orne; her only resort would be flight. If we could see the coaster's sails from our deck, we would be visible from hers. As I thought this, I could see the patch of white change direction; she had sighted us and was either wearing or tacking to escape. "Mr. Smythe," I shouted, "shake out the tops'ls!" Under the impetus of the extra canvas, we forged after the prize, hoping to intercept her quickly. We were much the faster ship and narrowed the gap rapidly. As we reached her, I could make out the chase; it was a large lugger with a single topsail. The ship must have been somewhere between eighty and one hundred tons, but I could not tell for sure in the dim light. "Mr. Buckley!"

"Aye, sir."

"Fire the bow chaser. Put one across her."

The short 9-pounder in the bow stood on a specially reinforced section of deck. If the area had not been built up, the ship would have been too weak for the gun. It fired, a sharp retort echoing throughout the ship and bouncing off the nearby cliffs of the shore. At the blast of the cannon, the lugger let her lugsail fly. We had been successful with just the threat of violence. Taking a prize should have some therapeutic effect on the crew; it is difficult to be sullen and count up your share of prize money at the same time. I was not surprised at the easy surrender; a lugger that size would have a crew of four or five men and if they carried any guns, it would be just a couple of swivels. As I thought this, I realized that my thinking was fallacious:

luggers no larger than this were frequently used as privateers. Armed with two to six guns and crammed with as many men as we had on the brig, they were bad news for any merchant ship they sighted. When we boarded the prize, we would have to make sure that it was a merchantman, not a privateer.

I called for the gig to be lowered. Taking a brace of pistols from Murphy, I made sure that every man on the gig's crew was armed with a pistol or blunderbuss in addition to a cutlass or boarding ax. This was our first prize. I decided to board her myself, taking Mr. Midshipman Dinsdale with me. Before leaving I warned Mr. Buckley about the possibility of trouble, saying, "Stand to the guns 'till we're sure she's not a privateer."

Our precautions were unnecessary; the lugger was a merchantman with a crew of five, counting her captain. I saw to the locking of the Frenchmen in the lugger's hold, then quickly checked the supplies and manifests. Finding a large number of full wine bottles in the captain's cabin, I had those sent to the *Rapid* to be put into my cabin stores. It would have been foolish to leave them aboard as a temptation to the prize crew. The wine never would have reached England; if it were left aboard, the prize crew might never reach England too, for they would be drunk before they were out of sight of the brig. After sending the wine back to the sloop, I looked for and found the manifests. The lugger, the *Colombe Blanche*—the *White Dove*—was loaded with rice and millet. The rice would sell very well in England, but I didn't know what kind of market there was for millet. In fact, other than realizing that it was some kind of grain, I didn't know what it was. I found out later that millet was used for bird food, but was edible for humans too. Since all but two hundred weight of the cargo was rice, I didn't worry about the value of the bird seed.

A prize crew would have to be detached from the brig to sail the *Dove* to England. Both of my midshipmen were inexperienced and did not know how to navigate; I hoped that they could box the compass, but even if they couldn't one of the seamen would be able to show them the trick. At first I thought of sending Mr. Buckley back; if he were ill, he could recover in England. He managed to convince me that he would not have a recurrence of his fit. Sailing a boat to England should be simple. They only had to sail west across the Channel. I failed to see any way they could not make it home. As Young Dinsdale had come over to the prize with me, I decided to put him in charge. "Pass the word for Mr. Dinsdale," I said. A few minutes later, he was on the quarterdeck of the *Dove*. He seemed out of breath and still looked frightened of me. "Mr. Dinsdale," I told him, "you will take charge of the prize. Hobbs and Dawson will go with you. Sail due west until you sight England."

"Aye aye, sir," he piped, and then broke wind loudly.

Poor Dinsdale, whenever he was excited or frightened, he practically fired a twenty-one-gun salute. I was not sad to see him go, for the quarterdeck of the prize had become an unpleasant place to stand. I left it to check the captain's cabin again. I was hoping to find a sextant or quadrant, but since the Frenchman was engaged in coasting, he carried neither. They were not necessary if the man kept the shore in sight. "Murphy!" I called, "make the gig ready for us to return."

"Aye aye, sair," he said.

Before leaving, I made sure that Dinsdale had the correct compass course. "Godspeed, Mr. Dinsdale," I told him.

He looked very proud and puffed out his frail chest. "Thank you, sir." I noticed that he seemed a little less frightened of me.

I regained my ship and watched the *Dove* make a westing away from us. God grant her a safe passage home. I ordered the sloop to wear and we headed back to the estuary of the Orne. Possibly another French ship would either leave or try to enter the river before the night was over. We took our station and hove to by the wind. As dawn began to break, the hills and beaches of the French coast became visible. From up at the masthead came the lookout's shout, "Deck, there. Sail ho!" A small string of coasters, three of them in all, were waiting for enough light to cross the bar and enter the river. They didn't have a chance, but one of them tried to run while we boarded the other two. The sloop was off in hot pursuit; after a short chase, we fired a warning shot. The coaster hove to without further protest.

The problem I had foreseen earlier was at hand. Mr. Dinsdale was gone; he was in command of the lugger. I assigned Mr. Hornswoggler to a sloop-rigged vessel of about seventy-five tons. This ship carried a cargo of cheese and butter which should prove very valuable. Before letting Hornswoggler depart, I surreptitiously removed one firkin of butter and a wheel of cheese from the vessel. Everything aboard a captured ship should remain for the prize auction, but in practice a little was often skimmed off the top. I had no other midshipmen, so I was forced to assign the other two ships to the only master's mates aboard the *Rapid*. Mr. Bryan Rummage was sent off with a cargo of Lisle silk and Mr. Tyson Lewis took command of the last prize, a small ketch loaded with salted pork. Eight men, two officers, and two petty officers had now been detached for prize duty. With a crew as small as ours, this was a serious depletion. Since England was close, I would sail to pick the men up, but resolved to cruise for another day or so in hope of winning yet another prize.

By the time the last of the prizes had left for England, the sun was well up. The day was bright, the sky cloudless. There was enough wind for little white caps to be skirling about the water's surface. It was a grand day; it was a glorious day; it was a most auspicious day. The crew, each and every man of them, seemed to be smiling a welcome to the sun. As I had surmised, the thought of prize money had dispelled the gloomy spirits, the sullen mood of the crew. We had done a good night's work; the bonus of prize money should equal more than a year's pay for each and every seaman.

While waiting for breakfast to be served, I gazed upward and watched the sea birds make tracks against the empty azure sky. We were near land; I saw gulls, pelicans, and a lonely albatross. The morning meal was now served. Not having my own cook, I usually ate the same food the crew was served. Today the cook had taken extra trouble. The oatmeal porridge had been sweetened with molasses and since I had given most of the firkin of butter to the cook for use by the crew, each serving of the cereal had been embellished with a large gob of sweet, yellow butter. As each mess attendant had his mess kid filled to bring back to his mates, he added to the joy by saying, "Plum duff and fresh cheese today." The cook was in good spirits too; he also received prize money.

I did not begrudge the men the plum duff or their good spirits. I would enjoy both myself. My share of the prize money was larger than the share of any other aboard. When it came to the duff, I was looking forward to a generous slice. A duff was a flour pudding made by boiling the ingredients in a bag. When the cook was able to add dried plums or raisins, it was especially popular. The men sweetened it further with lavish helpings of molasses. Plum duff was a prime favorite with seamen everywhere; I was no exception.

As I ate my porridge, I thought about the problem of navigating ships back to the prize court. The compass was the main instrument of course and most seamen could box the compass. The latitude a ship sailed upon could be important too. We had no extra sextants aboard the *Rapid* and unless we were able to find one on a prize and appropriate it, we would have none but mine and the three belonging to the other officers. I could not afford to buy even quadrants, but I remembered that before the sextant was invented, a seamen had been able to determine the latitude by a crude device called a mariner's staff. If a prize crew were blown off course by a violent Channel storm, such a device might save the ship.

After breakfast, the men were lined up on the deck in a formation reminiscent of the church services aboard the *Monmouth*. It was neither Sunday, nor was this a service. I stood at the edge of the quarterdeck, looking down at the assemblage. "Men," I began, "we have taken our first prizes. As you saw, we were hard put to find navigators to sail them to England. If our prizes cannot be condemned, we will get no prize money. I'm sure that each and every one of you has already calculated the approximate amount due him for this morning's work." The crew started to smile. Nothing, absolutely nothing, can make a crew as happy as prize money. "To make sure that our captures reach a port, an English port rather than a French one, we will be conducting classes in basic navigation for every seaman who wishes to learn. Knowledge of these techniques is needed to qualify for master's mate. Even more important than future promotion, you will be able to sail a prize to wherever it can be converted to prize money.

Those of you wishing to join the class, contact Mr. Nutley. Dismissed!"

While the men were circling around talking to each other, or returning to work, or signing up with the bosun, I passed the word for the carpenter. "Chips, can you whittle out some mariner's staffs?"

"Aye, sir, I can."

"Fine, Chips, see to it right away."

"Aye aye, sir."

At noon the next day it seemed as if every seaman not on watch was trying to sight the sun with his primitive equipment. Mr. Smythe, the master, was busy showing them how to adjust the cross bar and read off the inclination of the sun over the horizon. My speech had produced the desired effect. Soon we would have an ample number of men who could take charge of a prize. I wondered for a few seconds if any of the prize crews would run when they reached England, but decided that most of them would not. With the prospect of prize money, they would stay.

We cruised the Bay of the Seine for two more days, but found no more fat prizes for our taking. The time I had allotted was up. We wore ship and sailed for Portsmouth, hoping to pick up the crews of our prizes there.

Chapter 14

The *Rapid* lay at anchor in the harbor at St. Peter Port, Guernsey. The ancient battlements of the stone fort looked down from the hill upon the ships at anchor there. Old though the fort was, the 24-pounders and 32-pounders emplaced there were a deterrent to French invasion of the island. Why Guernsey was British was a puzzle, but despite the fact that the native language was French, the currency French, English, or their own, and their location just off the coast of France, the Channel Islanders stubbornly supported King George. Many of the Islanders were seafaring men. The British Navy had many officers born in these islands who bore typically French names. I had heard that the islands were originally part of William the Conqueror's domain before he became King of England; the islands remained loyal to their duke even after Normandy reverted back to France. Jerseymen and Guernseymen were British and proud of it.

It was the end of June; we had been cruising the coast of France for almost two months. By lying in wait off the entrances to likely harbors, we had surprised many enemy vessels engaged in the coasting trade. For the most part, they were small, some as small as twenty tons; others ranged up to two hundred tons. Underarmed, undermanned, each and every one, they had put up little resistance. The ships were small, but they were all filled with cargo vital to France's well-being. Each was a blow against the French Government, the Directory. As the old nursery rhyme went:

> For want of a nail, the shoe was lost,
> For want of a shoe, the horse was lost.
> For want of . . . the kingdom was lost!

The ships were small, but each and every one taken helped weaken the enemy. The cumulative effect was not small, nor was the accumulated prize money. The crew, no longer sullen, skylarked whenever they had a chance. They responded to orders cheerfully and kept the sloop spotless. Even Lieutenant Buckley seemed over his despondency, but I still worried that he might again have a fit. In all, things appeared to be going well. Mr. Yates, that dour Welsh surgeon, proved himself. He took excellent care of the men, remained sober, and did not hand out religious tracts. We had captured over thirty small enemy ships, but the only casualties during this period were O'Brien, a seaman who hit his head against a deck beam while drunk, and Jack Aubrey, the cook, who had burned himself when a pot of pea soup overturned.

Guernsey is an island, a small island. No sweeter words ever were told to the captain of one of His Majesty's ships. On a small island, the men couldn't run. Since they had nowhere to go, it was safe to give them shore leave. I wasn't worried about deserters, for the seaman who would run with a large amount of prize money due him is a *rara avis* indeed. No, rather than give up their share most men would put up with far worse than me. Prize money is a bar-

baric-sounding system, but no finer incentive to the spirit
and loyalty of a crew was ever devised. When all the claims
were adjudicated, each and every man aboard the *Rapid*
would receive a handsome sum. Most of them would spend
it caterwauling after women and rum, for a seaman and his
money are soon parted. A few would save it to invest in a
snug little inn somewhere in England. The dream of most
seamen, common seamen, is to become an admiral of the
blue by donning the blue apron of a publican. With their
own tavern, they would never have to worry about running
out of beer or spirits. I too was pleased with the amount of
prize money I had coming, but the game had begun to pall
on me. The merchant ships offered so little resistance that
I felt like a highwayman shouting, "Stand and deliver!"

The brothels and taverns of St. Peter Port welcomed my
crew with open arms. I did not find it necessary to visit
even the flossier officers' cribs, for while taking care of pur-
chasing fresh vegetables for the ship, I met a woman. She
was a wealthy widow, who surprised me by being five years
older than I. To look at her, one would have sworn her to
be much younger. She was small, elfin, slim, and dark-
haired, but then so are many women. As a description, that
leaves much to be desired, but how does one describe a
sunbeam refracting through a piece of old glass. *The Song
of Songs* comes closest to capturing her essence:

> *Thou art beautiful, O my love, as*
> *Tirzah,*
> *Comely as Jerusalem,*
> *Terrible as an army with banners.*
> . . . .
> *The joints of thy thighs are*
> *like jewels,*

The work of the hands of a cunning
workman.

. . . .

Thy two breasts are like two young roes
That are twins.

. . . .

How fair and how pleasant art
thou . . .

Marie Tallant, for that was her name, was vivacious at times, regal at others. When she smiled, her smile enfolded me as if I were entwined in her arms. Her late husband had been a naval officer; he died of the fever in the West Indies. She invited me to lunch with her. Once she had smiled at me, I would have followed her anywhere, like a puppy hoping to become a lap dog. I hastily concluded my purchases and arranged for the fruits and vegetables to be sent to the brig; I left the market with Marie and walked to her house.

It was a large house, built of great stone blocks. I did not notice the furnishings other than they pleased the eye and appeared rich. The luncheon was good, at least it was enjoyable; I do not remember what we ate. After the food, I relaxed with a glass of wine and we talked; I talked and she listened. Marie was that unusual person, a good listener. Before I knew it, I had told her all my fears and my aspirations. I drank considerable wine, but it wasn't the alcohol that loosened my tongue, it was she. In her company the time passed so quickly that when supper was served, it caught me unaware. After her servant cleared away the dishes, we went to yet another room where she played the harpsichord.

In the roseate glow of the candles, she appeared even more entrancing, if possible. I was completely enamored. I

could no more have left her house and company than I
could have surrendered my ship to an inferior force. We
wound up in her bed, naturally, as if we had been planning
it the entire day. I hadn't contrived her seduction; I had
only hoped. She proved as great a hoyden in bed as she had
been a lady in the drawing room. When at last we finished,
it was too late to sleep; it was 4:00 A.M. I had to leave for
the quay at five. We spent that last hour talking, kissing,
and just holding each other. I would never forget that
night, but I hoped to add a few others to it. As we parted,
I promised to stop and see her every time we were near
Guernsey. The *Rapid* was leaving that night, on the ebb,
for though St. Peter Port was a nice place to be, if we were
to harry the French, the crew and I would have to say good-
by to its fleshly delights and return to sea.

As the bells signaling the start of the first watch were
struck, the last of the shore-leave party to return under
their own power came aboard. The eight bells signified
midnight. I would have loved to have returned to Marie's
house, but the ebb was due in three hours. We would sail
then. I ordered a nose count; we were three men short.
There was still time to search them out and return them to
the ship instead of marking a "R" after their names to
show that they had deserted. I sent young Hornswoggler
ashore with a detail to visit the various bordellos, bagnios,
gambling dens, buttock's shops, and taverns in search of
the missing men. I was sure that they had not run. Two
hours later, a good hour before we were due to hoist
anchor, he was back with the three wretches who had over-
stayed their leave. Two of them were dead drunk, uncon-
scious, unable to locomote. The third, a satyr, was too
wrapped up in paying his respects to Miss Brown to
realize that the time for returning to the ship had passed.

An inspection of the ship turned up numerous bottles of rum that had been smuggled aboard by the seamen and three bottles of geneva. Rum is rum, so the contents of those were poured into a half-empty barrel for issue at a later date. The gin I sent to my cabin. I was not surprised to find no brandy. Brandy is a French tipple, too Frenchified for my British Jacks to drink. I remembered the time Pellew was forced to issue captured French brandy; we had finished all the rum aboard. For two days, the seamen groused and complained as if their spirit ration had been stopped. Given a choice, the Englishman preferred rum; given the opportunity the British seaman would drink anything. When the rum bottles were empty, I had them stowed below in the hold. We would be stopping French fishermen for fresh fish and information. Corked, empty bottles would be a much appreciated gift; they made excellent floats for fish nets.

Six bells, I thought, as the brazen notes rang through the ship. The ebb tide was due in less than fifteen minutes. "Prepare to hoist anchor!" I shouted. All sober hands were on deck or aloft. The great anchor cables were pulled through the hawsepipes by the capstan as the nippers dropped the cable in the cable tier. With the anchor catted home, the sails were set and we left St. Peter Port, heading for the open sea. The operation of getting under way was over; soon the dawn would break. If our cruise were successful, I would have to sail for England again, for once more we were short of seamen. The total number now aboard the *Rapid* was fifty-six, counting officers.

It was still dark when the bosun, Mr. Nutley, approached the quarterdeck dragging a drunken seaman by the collar. "Nutley," I said, "who do you have there?"

"Hit's a stowaway, sir. A bleedin', blinkin' stowaway. Can yer feature that?"

The man was very drunk, but he seemed capable of speech. He had been drinking with some of my men in a tavern. They had been bragging about their prize money. As a seaman on a merchant ship, the man, Parkinson, received better food, more living space, and a higher wage; the pay of naval seamen hadn't been raised since the time of Samuel Pepys and King James II. The past one hundred years had brought inflation, but seamen and officers too were still paid at the old rate. However, the merchant seaman wasn't in a position to get prize money. For all that matter, not every navy man was the recipient of such largesse. Prize money was a lure; it was always a possibility, but not always a certainty. Inflamed by his desire to share in such a bonus, Parkinson had jumped ship and stowed away on the *Rapid*. It wasn't often that a merchant seaman volunteered to join the king's service, but as far as I was concerned, he wouldn't get a chance to change his mind. "Mr. Nutley, this gentleman, Mr. Parkinson, wishes to join us. Give him the king's shilling and sign him up."

I chuckled as the bosun led the man away. John Parkinson was the name he claimed; it might well be his own, for Parkinsons were a rarer breed than the Joneses. That already numerous tribe is continually swelled by adoption; we had six who called themselves Jones aboard the brig. Jones or Parkinson, a prime seaman is a prime seaman; if the man had said, "Call me Ishmael," I would have signed him up under that name. I was glad to get him, only regretting that he was alone.

The sun was now up, hanging low in the east. The rays hit the water at an acute angle, causing the white caps to shimmer like polished white jade and the water itself to look like green nephrite. We sailed around the hoop of the bay, our compass needle flickering from south by west to south; we were heading toward Ushant and Brest. Once

there, I planned to cruise the ever dangerous Bay of Biscay.
The bay was a breeding ground of storms and shifting,
veering winds. There were many harbors and inlets, but the
shore line between these refuges was rocky. The waves lap-
ping at the beaches concealed reefs and rocks beneath the
water, ever ready to rip the bottom out of a ship. The bay
should prove to be a fertile hunting ground for French
coasters. We had started our cruise in the Bay of the Seine,
but after two weeks there had transferred our operations to
the Bay of Biscay, where the pickings had proven much
richer. We had left the area twice; once we had picked up
our prize crews at Portsmouth, the other time we had gone
to Guernsey for fresh vegetables and to allow the men a
run ashore. Now we were going back for the third time.

It was noon. The watches were changing. Up on the
quarterdeck, Mr. Smythe was conducting a lesson in navigation. His pupils were the two midshipmen. I left the
weather side and wandered over to listen in and see how
the boys were doing. Mr. Hornswoggler, as usual, looked
more mournful than a sin eater at a funeral. He had taken
his cocked hat off and the wind was ruffling his long, dank
hair. Mr. Dinsdale still wore his hat, but something about
his uniform looked strange. I looked closer and realized
that Dinsdale was growing. His jacket cuffs with the white
tabs did not reach all the way to his hand; they exposed
considerable wrist. Wearing breeches, as he was, I would
not have been able to see a gap between his shoes and cuff,
for breeches end at the knee and long stockings cover the
remainder of the legs. His coat rode high over his hips.
There was no question about it, the boy was growing. He
would have to spend some of his prize money on a new
uniform.

As I watched, I saw a funny expression on Smythe's face;

he sniffed, I followed suit. There was a foul odor on the quarterdeck; the stench was most offensive. "Mr. Dinsdale!" Smythe shouted, looking the boy square in his eyes. Dinsdale was just about as tall as Smythe. The midshipman became very nervous. He broke wind loudly, firing a regular volley as he was wont to do when he was upset. "Mr. Dinsdale," said Smythe again, "there was no need for you to repeat your offense."

"But, sir, I didn't." Whatever Dinsdale was about to say was interrupted by a loud explosion as he farted again.

I was watching Hornswoggler closely. His expression was just too innocent. I realized that the first stench had not been Dinsdale but Hornswoggler, who must have passed gas silently, hoping to have it blamed on the younger midshipman. To embarrass our practical joker, I said, "Mr. Hornswoggler, if you have to visit the head, I'm sure that Mr. Smythe would excuse you." Hornswoggler turned red, cochineal red, and looked most abashed. I had wounded him in his pride by exposing him, but I didn't think it a dramatic enough lesson to stop him from more pranks.

As the brig of war rounded Ushant, the lookout spotted a sail. "Ahoy deck," he shouted, "I sees a sail; it's a big 'un, looks like a frigate. She be dead ahead." We continued on our course, sailing ever closer to the unknown ship. When we were close enough to make it out, I would know what to do. If it should turn out to be French, I was confident that we were swift enough to show them our stern transom disappearing over the horizon; the *Rapid* lived up to her name. I was very alert, keyed up, ready to run if necessary, when the lookout shouted again. "Deck there, I recognizes 'er; it's the *Indy*."

I wondered how the man recognized the frigate *Indefatigable*, one of England's strongest. The ship had been a two-decker 64, but just recently had been cut down to a single deck to make a forty-four-gun frigate. Once a seaman knows a ship it is almost impossible for any changes to hide her identity. The *Indy* had retained her original masts and yards; possibly this was what made her recognizable to the lookout. Without recourse to the book, I knew who was in command of the frigate; it was Sir Edward Pellew, my old commander. We had parted company, I to go to my first post as a lieutenant, he to take command of the powerful new frigate. "Run up the recognition signals and make our number," I said.

The old *Indy* answered our signal and we continued our course to intercept her. Sir Edward was on deck; I recognized him immediately. As we pulled alongside, we hove to with less than a ship's width between us. I doffed my hat and shouted, "Sir Edward, a good morning to you, sir."

"Hullo, St. John," answered my old chief. "Do you have any news for us?"

"No, sir," I replied, "we're just in from St. Peter Port. I'm under independent orders. I shall be returning to England in the next two or three weeks. If you wish, I'll try to search you out then and see if you wish me to deliver any dispatches."

"Capital idea, St. John. Please do so if you're able. The French fleet is still inactive and apt to remain so unless we have a storm come up. You and your cockleshell should have good hunting unless the weather changes."

Leaving the *Indefatigable*, we continued our journey south past Ushant. Shortly after leaving the *Indy* we saw and spoke other British ships, the frigates *Revolutionare*, *Amazon*, *Phoebe*, and a small armed lugger, *Duke of York*. These three frigates, the flagship *Indefatigable* and the little *Duke* comprised the inshore squadron blockading the

French fleet. The squadron was under the command of Pellew, the senior captain.

When we spoke the lugger, I ordered my gig lowered and had myself rowed to her. Mr. Sparrow, her lieutenant commanding, was a friend. Since we both held the same rank, there was no cause of friction between us. I had thought the *Rapid* insignificant, but compared to Sparrow's command, a mighty fortress was my ship, especially since we had mounted the carronades. After a pleasant visit with Mr. Sparrow, I returned to the brig, ready to resume my cruise. It was nice to have an independent command. The inshore squadron had to keep station off Brest waiting for the French fleet. If the French did come out, Pellew and his frigates would have to shadow them and send word to the main British fleet. While they worked at holding the French Navy at bay, I was free to attack French commerce.

Chapter 15

A light mist shrouded the French coast. The *Rapid* was hove to by the wind a good two cables from the shore. The sun was up already and promising soon to burn the mist away, restoring our vision. It was a full day, the next morning, since we had spoke the *Indy*. A lookout had been sent to the top of each mast to search out potential victims for our net, but the low-hanging mist limited our circle of vision. "Deck ahoy!" shouted the man from the foremast. The action of the sun had reduced the amount of fog. The lookout was above it and could see. "They's a ship comin' out of yon inlet!"

There was not much we could do except wait. When the ship was out of the harbor, we could chase her by following the lookout's directions. Until then we could only make ready. "Beat to quarters!" I said. While we waited, the sun continued to beat down on the mist, thinning it every minute. We hauled the braces to the backed foresail and got the brig under way. The lookout hailed and gave us the direction the strange ship was making. "Set her at due south," I told the helmsman. The chase was making west by north. We should intercept her on this course.

The mist had cleared enough for us to see the ship from the quarterdeck. She was a Jonathan schooner. There was no doubt in my mind as to the ship's country of origin. The sharp bow, the towering, sharply raked masts, even the way the ship was handled, shouted American. American or not, if she were coming out of a French harbor, the schooner had been trading with the enemy. The wind was blowing to the northeast, coming from our quarter. It was a head wind for the schooner, forcing the American to beat against the wind. We had the weather gauge; it was no contest, but if the wind had been in a different direction, and if the schooner had seen us, she could probably have walked away from us. We intercepted at about six bells of the morning watch. "Fire a shot across her bows!" I shouted.

At the shot, the American hove to. Rather than send Buckley or one of the midshipmen, I went over the side to the gig to lead the boarding party myself. I was sure that the ship would be a fair prize, for we had caught her red-handed trading with the enemy. I was wrong. Despite the fact that we had seen the schooner come out of a French port, we were unable to prove the charge. The ship was in ballast. Undoubtedly she had left a cargo back there, but as there were no French goods aboard her now, there was no way to disprove the American captain's story that he had stopped in the French harbor to make necessary repairs. Without documents to back my claim, I knew that any prize court would throw this case out. Angered by the loss of prize money, I ordered the American crew lined up to inspect the men. A few were obviously British. One in particular could only have developed his accent in England, but each man had a Protection Certificate made out and signed by the proper authorities. Some English captains would have pressed these men regardless, but I could see no sense in deepening the breach between the two countries.

"Captain Meacham," I told the grizzled old American salt, "I don't believe that the Protections are authentic, nor do I believe that you were making repairs and watering in France, but since we can't prove otherwise, I'm leaving you, your ship and crew intact."

"Wal, thank ye kin'ly, Cap'n," he said. "Yore ship is the *Rapid*, is it not?"

"Yes."

"Wal, sir, while I was waterin', I heard some talk 'bout you an' yore ship. The French think that ye be a damned pirate. They also say that ye be the de'il. Regardless of which ye be, they're plannin' t' git ye. I hear that a big corvette is a searchin' for ye."

"Thank you, Captain Meacham," I said, and then left his ship. So the French were disturbed enough by our recent captures to put a corvette out to search for me. I should have felt flattered, but I didn't. The frogs were searching for a small gun brig. If I could alter the appearance of the *Rapid*, they might ignore it, or if not they would react slower if they thought us to be a merchant ship. It was worth a try. I called for the carpenter and the sailmaker to join me. I suggested some changes; they agreed that they were feasible. I gave them their orders to complete the transformation.

A brig has two masts as does a snow, a schooner, and a brigantine. Rather than rig a trysail mast for the driver sail to become a snow, I had suggested converting the *Rapid* into a brigantine. A snow looks too much like a brig; it would be no disguise at all. Six hours later, His Majesty's brigantine, *Rapid*, 18, was ready for action. The square sails had been removed from the main mast and a taller driver sail substituted. Both top gallant masts had been sent down, leaving only main and topsails on the foremast. Two fore and aft sails now flew between the two masts where before we had only one. The entire profile of the *Rapid* was changed. Even from end on, the appearance would be different. As Mr. Nutley said after the transformation was completed, "Hit's a jackass brig, that's wha' hit is. A jackass brig don't look like no normal brig, hit looks peeculyar, like a goddamned 'maphrodite."

We poked our bow into the various bays and guts down the French shore line, but from Lorient to La Rochelle, no ships were moving. It's possible that the French coasters were huddled in their ports fearing the descent of the *Rapid*. If so, from a strategic point of view, our cruise was most successful. Successful strategy does not put prize money in the purse. The crew began to get edgy, but they were not sullen. Even Mr. Hornswoggler had given up his pranks to pace irritably up and down until he could control himself no longer. Then he would hurl himself aloft with a spyglass in hand to see if he could do better than the lookouts. He was at the cap of the foremast on the third day after we left Lorient. We were somewhere between the Île d'Oléron and the French coast above where the Charente River joins the sea. The river is the water road to Rochefort, in the French interior. "Deck there!" shouted Mr. Hornswoggler. "Sail ho!"

"Can you make it out?" I shouted back.

"Aye, sir. It's a ship; I can see all three masts."

I ran to the ratlines and started aloft. Opening my telescope, I focused on the ship. It seemed a fine ship, larger than any we had captured. I estimated it at close to four hundred tons. As we drew closer together, I revised my estimate upward; the vessel was at least six hundred tons. Since she had not turned to run when she saw us, I realized that this was no peaceful merchant. Only a man-of-war will head toward an unknown sail willingly. "Beat to quarters!"

I roared, and then started to descend to the deck. Horn-swoggler flashed past me, reaching the quarterdeck before I did.

The drummer started the rhythm of "Heart of Oak," his drumsticks flashing in the sunlight. The stick blows on the tightly stretched skin of the drumhead reverberated through the brig. The men hurried to their positions. If there was to be a battle, we must make ready. Partitions were knocked down and stowed below along with furniture and chests. The cook rushed to prepare a hot meal so the men could go into battle with full stomachs. As soon as the food was served, he would douse the galley fire and put the coals overboard. Guns were unshackled from their lash-up position, the decks sanded to prevent slipping on blood, and a net rigged above the deck to protect the men from falling objects. The hammocks were placed in their hammock nets; they could raise the height of the bulwark and offer some protection from the fire of snipers. In the fighting tops of the two masts, the monkey-tailed swivel guns were made ready. Since no match was allowed up near the sail, fresh gun flints were placed in each lock to ensure ignition of the powder. Muskets were made ready for use by the sharpshooters aloft too.

The men were fed; each mess attendant brought the mess kid back to the kitchen to clean while his mess mates set up tubs of water near each gun. The smaller contained fresh water for drinking; the larger held sea water to soak the "wooly-'eaded bastard," the lamb's wool sponger.

Mr. Buckley went from gun to gun, checking to see if all the accouterments were laid out ready to use. Each gun had a rammer, a sponge, a crowbar, priming quills, and slow match if the flintlock failed. The slow match was lighted and placed in notches of the large tub. The lighted end was over the water to prevent accidental fire. While

Buckley was checking the guns, the cook dumped the live coals from the galley fire over the side. A runner went to the magazine to inform Morris that the galley fire was out. It was now safe to send up the gunpowder cartridges. I ordered all the guns loaded. "Mr. Buckley, have all the broadside guns loaded with double ball and a charge of grape on top of that. Mr. Hornswoggler, I want the quarterdeck carronades loaded with a single ball and two bags of musket balls each." Knowing my orders would be carried out, I continued to plan my strategy. The *Rapid* was now ready, as ready as I could make her.

The strange ship started to wear and headed away from us, as if it had suddenly seen us and was running to safety. Perhaps I was wrong; it must be a peaceful merchant ship after all. On the other hand, it could be a stratagem to deceive us into thinking that it was not a man-of-war. When it came to the game of stratagems, two could play. I would have to be very careful. As the French ship bore away from us, some of the men started to cheer. They were counting their prize money already. "Silence!" I shouted. We were catching up to the other ship rather quickly. Either it was a slow sailer or they were lagging to allow us to overtake them. Up on the fo'c'sle Mr. Buckley had loaded the bow chaser; we were very close now. If she did not heave to when I fired the warning shot, I would tack across her stern and rake her. "You may fire now, Mr. Buckley."

"Fire!" he shouted. The 9-pounder discharged, reeling back with the explosive fury of its recoil. A cloud of dense white smoke wreathed the bow of the brigantine. The ship hauled her foreyards 'round and hove to. I looked for a flag to fall, but none had been run up the mast. Our guns were all run out, ready to fire. We sailed up alongside the other ship at closer than half-pistol length. Something was wrong; I could sense trouble, but could not tell what it was that alerted me. We started to heave to at my order. I was watching the French ship; the Tricolor flag started to rise at the foremast and I saw motion as the ship began to trice up the gun ports. Her captain would have done better to have fired right through the hatches. As the port covers started up, I shouted, "Fire!"

I saw the flash of Buckley's sword as he relayed my order to the portside battery. The gunners had been perfecting their aim as we pulled alongside the other ship. As I was shouting, "Belay the heave to," to the waisters, Buckley's gun captains released the cocks of their flintlocks, firing all seven of the broadside 24-pounders. Each gun roared and recoiled back against the snubbing ropes. The force of so many guns going off at once shook the *Rapid* as hard as if we had been broached by a high wave. The planks underfoot trembled and a dense cloud of choking, acrid smoke drifted away from our ship toward the enemy. With them to the lee, we would be able to see our target unobstructed by our own smoke. The carronades were quickly run in and loaded, run out and fired again.

Before the echo of the first broadside died out, the waisters had hauled the foresail yards and we were under way. As our bow passed the enemy's bow, I ordered the vessel tacked, telling the helmsman, "Steer small, damn it, steer small." We tacked across her beak, raking her with yet another broadside as we passed. I did not try to heave to in raking position, for if they got the ship under way again, she would climb up our side, allowing the French a chance to board us. They were already massing on their ship's bow, as we passed. As soon as the bow was dead abeam of our quarterdeck, I signaled Hornswoggler, who had the quarterdeck carronades fired. The musket balls swept through the massed men, cutting them down as a scythe mows grain; cutting them down into a screaming jumble of broken parts, as hundreds of one-ounce lead balls drove through their ranks. An officer, I could tell from the gold braid, who commanded the boarding party, was still standing. He raised his sword and shook it threateningly at us, but whatever he shouted, I could not hear over the din of the cannon or the screaming of the wounded.

I was in constant motion about my quarterdeck, knowing that a moving target is harder to hit. As we rounded the bow of the corvette, we fired another broadside, but this was answered by the French. Long tongues of flame lanced out of the muzzles of the enemy cannon, reaching, reaching out for me. I continued to pace up and down; young Dinsdale was dogging my footsteps, ready to carry an order for me if necessary. His face was tight and pale; he was terrified. So was I. I wondered about Lieutenant Buckley, but from the continued action of the broadside carronades, I hoped that he was still well. As I walked, the banshee shriek of balls passing overhead raised the hackles on the back of my neck. I had to keep my fear penned within, for if I looked afraid, I might panic my crew. The Frenchman was firing on the uproll. His balls were carrying high overhead. I saw one ball strike the foresail, splitting it open. Then a man came tumbling out of our mainmast, striking the protective net and bouncing off into the water. I looked up when he fell; the netting was littered with blocks and other tackle. If we had not rigged the net, some of these might have struck the men.

The carronades fired again, hitting the enemy ship and sending clouds of splinters flying through the air. A small puff of dust rising up from the deck caught my eye; it is not normal for dust to fall upward. Marksmen in the tops of the French corvette were firing muskets at the quarter-deck, at me. A sharp, yelping noise from our foremast indicated that the swivel gun in the fighting top had been fired. The main job of the gunners in the masts is to neutralize the enemy sharpshooters. At the sound of the swivel gun, two men, one still holding a musket banded with brass, pitched out of the Frenchman's rigging and fell to the deck below.

Hornswoggler served the enemy another helping of musket balls, this time topped with grape. His target had been the enemy quarterdeck. All who had stood there before his order to fire were now down, the corvette swinging wildly with no hands at the wheel. A Frenchman rushed to take the wheel, to put the ship back under control. It seemed an eternity since the fight had started, but the French had fired only two broadsides; we had fired six. Our guns went off again, arcing the heavy balls into the hull of the ship. "Swab out! Damn you, swab out!" I heard a gun captain scream to his gunners.

Once again the French fired. It was a ragged broadside; only half their guns fired. A ball came whistling across the quarterdeck directly at me. For a split second, I thought that the ball had made my number. I started to jump aside, but my reactions were too slow; the ball passed by without hitting me; it was close, but it missed. Young Dinsdale was right behind me when the ball passed. He fell to the deck in a crumpled heap. I was sorry to see the lad go. He was growing up; he would have made the king a fine officer, but now he was dead. To my surprise, he stood up a few seconds later. There were tears running down his face, but he resumed his station and continued to dog my steps. I learned later that the ball had not touched him, but the wind of its passage had been great enough to knock him sprawling. After missing Dinsdale, the missile struck the far bulwarks and sent a great cloud of slivers into the air.

The French flag started to flutter down, but before it

reached the deck a carronade went off with a tremendous blast. The French had struck; victory was ours. "Pass the word for Mr. Buckley," I said.

Someone, it was Dinsdale, ran to get the first lieutenant. He was back moments later, tears streaming down his face, cutting channels in the black, powder grime. "S-s-sir," he stammered, "Buckley's been killed."

Young Dinsdale had stood up to the ordeal of battle better than I had thought he would, especially after being knocked over by the wind of the ball that nearly killed him, but the death of Buckley was almost too much for him. I had to do something to keep him busy. "Mr. Dinsdale, go below and speak to Mr. Yates. Ask him for the butcher's bill, then report back to me."

I watched the midshipman disappear below; he was heading for the cockpit. With Buckley dead, I would have to send Mr. Hornswoggler off with the prize. He too was on the quarterdeck, standing next to his carronades. I was sure that he had overheard Dinsdale and knew about Buckley. He looked gloomy, but then I had never seen him look otherwise. "Mr. Hornswoggler, you will board the prize. Order the boats out."

"Aye aye, sir," he answered.

Poor Buckley gone; I would miss him. During the fight, the fire of the broadside guns had not slackened. I wondered when the lad had been hit, or if someone else had taken over the guns? If so, who? Dinsdale came up the ladder. He had moved quickly and was puffing with the exertion; it hadn't taken him long to go to the very bowels of the brig and return. "Sir," he blurted out, "Mr. Yates says that we have five dead and six wounded."

In so small a ship's company, that was a steep price indeed, a high butcher's bill. We had only forty-six effectives left unless some of the wounded were capable of limited service. That damned French corvette we had just captured probably had a ship's company of one hundred fifty or more. It would be a difficult job to guard all of those prisoners and man both ships with only forty-six men. There was much to be done. Hornswoggler was about to board the corvette. I watched as our boats were swung out. The jolly boat, which normally hung by davits on the stern, had been hit by a cannon ball; it could be repaired, but would be a difficult job. It was fortunate indeed that the gig and the two cutters, which were kept nested together between the masts, had not been hit. I still had to check the damage reports, make a plan of how to handle the prisoners, and find out what had happened on the gun deck when Buckley fell. Dinsdale was too emotional to send off on the latter errand; I sent him looking for the carpenter and the sailmaker. I spotted Murphy from where I stood—his red hair a beacon that couldn't be missed. "Murphy," I shouted, and my cox'n came running. "Murphy, nip down to the gun deck and find out when Mr. Buckley fell. If it was before the end of the battle, find out who took over the guns."

From what I could see of the ship, the French practice of firing on the up roll had saved the brig from serious damage. Many blocks had fallen on the netting; lines and shrouds had been cut by ball. These could be repaired quickly. I set those of the crew still aboard to repair the rigging. We had all of the carronades loaded, ready to fire if the French showed any signs of treachery.

The carpenter reported to me; there was some repair work to do on the bulwarks and a few shot holes to plug. None of the holes were below the water line. He left as the sailmaker came to report extensive damage to the rigging, but none that we couldn't fix. The brig was in relatively good condition.

I looked toward the prize. My men had boarded and were herding the prisoners down into the hold. They were offering no resistance. Those left on the deck were either dead or wounded. I saw a couple of my seamen start to pitch the dead Frenchmen over the side to clear the decks. They had started making repairs. We had fired on the down roll; most of our shot had hit the corvette in the hull or swept the decks. I could see some of the guns; they were overturned. I would have liked to go on board the prize myself, but I couldn't spare the men to row me there.

As I watched, I saw a few French officers and some *sous* officers herded down into one of our cutters. A party of my seamen dropped into the boat too. Mr. Ready, one of the bosun's mates, was in charge of the party. He held a pair of pistols in his hands as the Frenchmen were rowed to the *Rapid.* I couldn't hear what Ready said, but it must have been effective, for the Frenchmen, officers and petty officers alike, helped row the boat. The fact that Ready weighed eighteen stone and looked tough enough to eat the cutter for breakfast probably helped convince them to be co-operative. When they reached the brig, they were brought up and locked below. Hornswoggler had learned his lesson well. When taking a strong prize, always separate the officers from the men.

Since the boat was available, I decided to join Mr. Ready and go aboard the prize to see how Mr. Midshipman Hornswoggler was coping. By the time I climbed to the deck of the ship, all of the dead had been disposed of. The wounded had been taken to the cockpit where the French surgeon was doing his best. I decided to ask Mr. Yates to come over and help when he finished with our wounded, for the French had suffered so many casualties. Hornswoggler was on the quarterdeck; I climbed the ladder to join him. He nodded to me, then looked down at a sheaf of papers he held in his hand. "Sir, the prize is the French national corvette the *Dragonet*, 22. As you surmised, she was looking for us."

She had found us. Our disguise hadn't helped much. When we sailed directly for a ship of superior size, they knew that we were either a privateer or a king's ship. Possibly our disguise had made them think we were a privateer instead of the dreaded *Rapid*. "Very good, Mr. Hornswoggler," I said. "What else have you learned?"

"Her captain fell when we fired the canister. The second captain took over, but he was soon wounded. They took a frightful butcher's bill. I estimate the French loss at fifty-six killed and forty wounded from a crew of one hundred sixty."

"How soon will damages be repaired?"

"About three hours, sir. I've put the French sailmaker and carpenter to work."

"Very good. Mr. Hornswoggler, you will be in charge of the *Little Dragon*. Since we are so shorthanded, you must keep a close watch on your prisoners. We shall be shorthanded aboard the *Rapid* too, so we shall sail for Portsmouth together."

I returned to the brig to send Mr. Yates to the *Little Dragon*. Dinsdale was on the quarterdeck; he was limping and his face contorted with pain. "Have you seen Mr. Yates, Dinsdale?" I asked, wishing to be sure that the lad saw the surgeon before he left for the French ship.

"Aye, sir, I did. He said that the wind of the ball that knocked me over was so severe that it bruised me, bruised me all over."

"That is peculiar, Mr. Dinsdale. I shall have to speak to Mr. Yates about you. Perhaps, I can even write a paragraph or two about the effect of the wind of a cannon ball upon the human body. I'm sure that the *Gazette* will publish it."

Chapter 16

The repairs to the prize completed, it was time to set sail for England and the prize court. We had too few seamen aboard either the *Little Dragon* or the *Rapid*. If we were attacked by an enemy, any enemy, I feared for the results; even a rowboat armed with but a single swivel could give us a battle. I just had to hope and pray that we would not encounter any French ship on our voyage. If we did, I might have to abandon the prize and burn it. Setting the *Little Dragon* afire would be a problem, for there were over one hundred Frenchmen penned below decks; I couldn't cremate them alive. I would have to solve that problem and solve it soon.

Looking about the deck for a midshipman, I saw none. I remembered that other than the master and myself, young Dinsdale was the only officer left aboard the brig. "Pass the word for Mr. Dinsdale," I told Murphy as he brought me a hot cup of tea and a ship's biscuit.

"Aye aye, sir," he said, and disappeared to search out the midshipman.

From habit, I knocked the biscuit against the rail. The vibrations produced by tapping would annoy the weevils, if they were present, and they would leave the bread. I should have known better, for the bread was fresh. We had purchased a new store in Guernsey. Murphy, who had a tendency to mother me, had made sure that my private stock of ship's bread was replaced with fresh; there were no weevils. I dunked the biscuit into the hot tea to soften it and started to eat. As I took my first bite, Mr. Dinsdale came limping to the poop. "Ahahh, young Dinsdale," I said. "I wish you to send a signal to the prize." He hobbled over to the flag locker and started hooking signal flags to a halliard. Soon the preparatory signal was hoisted; then the signal to make sail. Both vessels were under way, heading to England.

We had been sailing for almost three hours, beating against the wind, when we approached the Île d'Yeu. There were several French fishing boats working nets just to the west of the island. Since warships normally do not bother fishermen, they did not run, but continued netting. The fishing fleet could be an answer to my problem. Signaling to the prize, we headed for the fishermen. The Frenchmen were willing to accept some of our money in exchange for fish and lobster, but when I suggested that they relieve us of the prisoners, they were not too happy. They would be forced to go in early, for so many men would crowd their vessels. "Monsieur, if the prisoners are not taken, I will sink your boats one at a time until you decide to comply." The Frenchman I addressed myself to did not seem to believe me. "Mr. Dinsdale," I shouted, "load and run out one carronade." When the ugly, black snout of the cannon was poked out of the gun port, the fishermen decided to be more co-operative. We turned over all of the French seamen, keeping only the unwounded officers to take back to England. Off-loading the wounded was a problem, but by use of nets and slings, the injured were lowered to the decks of the fishing boats. It would have been better to have taken all of the Frenchmen to England

where they could have been put in prison; that would ensure that they would not again serve against us, but the risk
of holding them with so shorthanded a crew was too great.
With no prisoners aboard, Mr. Hornswoggler would not
have to worry about an attempt to take back the ship. It
also settled the moral question of burning the prize if it became necessary for us to abandon it.

We left the fishermen and continued our voyage. The
thought of fresh lobster at dinner was most pleasant to
contemplate. I still had some butter left that we had
picked up in Guernsey; fine Guernsey butter as good as the
best from Hampshire or Devon. It was still sweet and fresh,
I knew, for I had used some at breakfast that morning. The
cook would draw the lobster and serve it with melted butter and a little lemon juice from the anti-scorbutic cask. I
licked my lips and almost drooled in anticipation. I had
purchased several of the lobsters for my own use; they were
alive, swimming in a barrel of sea water. I would be able to
have the same meal several times, or I could invite the only
officers present aboard the brig for dinner. It would be the
civil thing to do, I decided. If one of the master's mates
took the watch, both Dinsdale and the master could attend. Mr. Yates would be invited too, of course. I was still
thinking about the dinner party when Mr. Midshipman
Dinsdale came up on the quarterdeck. It felt strange to
leave him with the ship, but he had to assume responsibility sooner or later. I left and went to my cabin where I
would be available if needed.

Murphy was in the cabin, straightening out my few
belongings. It was an odd time for him to be there for that
purpose, so I realized that he was using it only as an excuse
to talk with me. "Yes, Murphy," I said.

"Sair, you asked me to check what happened when Mr.

Buckley fell; Oi did. It was Fry, the gunner's mate, who took over when Buckley was kilt."

I had made Fry an assistant gunner's mate after I saw him talking to one of the carronades. Fry, a big Cornishman, was entirely too bovine a type to have taken command of the guns, or so I had thought. It seemed that this Mr. Fry had hidden talents. I learned later that Fry was so enamored of the big guns that he watched every step Mr. Buckley made and memorized every order. When Buckley was killed, Fry had no difficulty in taking his place. Such initiative should be rewarded, but I wasn't sure how to do so. Fry was a big, fat, sloppy man who looked almost half-witted. It would be difficult to get him promoted. The best thing I could do for the man would be to give him a golden guinea.

Two days later, both ships were still keeping company. We were not far from the Lizzard when the ever unpredictable Atlantic whipped up a storm. With too few men to handle the sails, I resolved to ride out the weather under a balanced mizzen. I ordered my intentions signaled to the prize; we had to spell out much of the message for the signal code did not contain all the words.

The storm was soon upon us. It was a summer storm, a thunderstorm. The air grew black and close; it was difficult to breathe. Great gouts of rain fell; lightning flashed; the wind roared. "Drop both anchors!" I shouted. It was easy to shout, but my order could not be complied with immediately. The anchors were not at the catheads; they were stowed below. Mr. Nutley and a group of men had to horse them up and cat them to the bow. The cables had to be bent to each anchor. When they were ready, the bosun took a maul and struck the anchor release pins. First the starboard and then the port anchor were dropped to plummet down to the water; each raised a mighty splash and started sinking toward the bottom, sinking down, down, down to the end of the cable. There was no bottom. The weight of the anchors and cables slowed our drift, but we were still making lee. If we could not stop drifting, we would wind up aground on the Cornish coast, a fair prey for the ship wreckers of Cornwall. I ordered the sailmaker to make a large, funnel-shaped drogue anchor of canvas and stream it out from the stern of the *Rapid*. When it was completed, they dropped it in the water. Would it work? I could only pray that it would. The drogue drifted out behind the brig to the end of its line where, with no slack left, it stiffened; the water pushing against the canvas held us; we were still making some lee, but the action of the drogue had turned us. We were no longer drifting toward the inhospitable rocks.

The ship under control at last, I stood on the quarterdeck, drenched. A bolt of lightning struck the foremast, dancing around the iron bands reinforcing the mast. The lightning circled the mast like a corona of fire, then leaped to the deck where the planking started to smolder. If it had not been raining so hard, we probably would have caught fire, but the oak only smoked and smoldered until it was completely doused with a couple of leather buckets of sea water.

As storms do, this one passed; we stopped pitching. It was now a calm sea, a sea so calm it looked like a mill pond after the race was shut off. I ordered the anchors hoisted. Practically every man on the *Rapid* had to work the capstan as the big fourteen-inch cables were snaked back aboard. When we had dropped the anchors, they had gone out the hawsepipes so quickly that they smoked and produced a stench of hemp. Hoisting the cables back inboard was much slower.

I had sent a lookout—I could only afford to spare one

man—to the mast top to look for the *Little Dragon*. She was nowhere in sight. I hoped that Hornswoggler had been able to ride out the storm too. I was worried about him; an inexperienced youngster on a shorthanded ship, he might well have been wrecked. I kept the lookout aloft; it was possible that he might see our prize or her wreck shortly.

"Sail ho!" shouted the seaman from the masthead. I wondered if it were Hornswoggler, but my unspoken question was soon answered. "It ain't the *Dragon*, sir." The ship was a good five miles off. I didn't know if it were friend or foe, but with so few seamen aboard, I didn't propose to find the answer. Since we did not have enough men to fight, I decided to run. I ordered all possible sail made. We were chased for three hours. With the stun sails out and the top gallants in place, the *Rapid* was fast, but as fast as we were, the strange sail determinedly hung on, neither losing nor gaining. As we were in the Channel, I hoped that a British ship would intervene. I stared back at our pursuer over the taffrail. Was he gaining? It was hard to be sure, but it looked as if the sail were growing larger. It was a good thing the prize was no longer with us, or I would have been forced to set it ablaze and call the prize crew back aboard the *Rapid* to help us fight. The lookout shouted again, "I thing 'e's the *Nymphe*, I does."

The *Nymphe* had been my first ship. I jumped up into the ratlines and made my way hurriedly to the top. When I reached the futtock shrouds, I decided to go through the lubber's hole rather than hang upside down like a sloth just to impress the crew that I could make the climb. Once in the fighting top, I opened my telescope. The man was right; it was His Majesty's frigate, *Nymphe*, 36. I leaned over the rail enclosing the top and shouted down to the deck. "Send up our number and the recognition signal." The flags went fluttering up the halliard to be answered by an eruption of color on the masts of the frigate. The flags confirmed the fact that it was one of ours. The number she displayed was that of the *Nymphe*, but one couldn't be too careful. "Beat to quarters!" I shouted. "Load all the guns and run out." If the frigate should prove to have been captured, we would be as ready as we could when she came up to us. I ordered sail taken in to slow our speed.

As the *Nymphe* came up alongside, I picked up my black, japanned, tin speaking trumpet and prepared to hail her as we hove to. "Lt. Sinjin, Commander, His Majesty's brig of war, *Rapid*, 18," I shouted. "Have you seen either a ship or a wreck?"

The figure on the quarterdeck of the frigate raised his trumpet. "Captain Melville, His Majesty's ship of war, *Nymphe*, 36. Did you say brig? It looks like a hermaphrodite." He paused to laugh. I couldn't blame him, the jackass rig of a brigantine would look strange to any navy captain. If we had not been shorthanded, I would have changed it back, but with so few men aboard, it was a blessing. The brigantine required fewer men to man the sails than the brig. "Lieutenant St. John," he said, "yours is the first vessel I have seen since the storm broke."

I thanked Captain Melville. Since it was possible that he would run into Hornswoggler and the *Little Dragon*, I decided to ask him to pass a message if he did. "The ship was the *Dragonet*, 22, a French national corvette. She was our prize, but we parted company in the storm. If you should see her and speak her, please tell them that the *Rapid* is undamaged."

Melville looked incredulous. "You captured a twenty-two-gun corvette with this, this jackass brig? By Jove, sir, that sounds like a fine prize."

As he envied our luck in capturing the corvette, I looked at him and envied him his station. The man wore a single epaulette like me, but he wore his on the right shoulder, the opposite shoulder from the one that bore my epaulette.

He was a post captain; he was on the list. Once a man had
been posted, he was secure in his profession. He had only
to outlive those ahead of him on the list to become an admiral. I envied him the trim, sleek frigate with its thirty-six
guns. He was young to have such a fine ship. Perhaps he
was the favorite of some powerful admiral. With an 18-
pounder frigate like his, I would have been willing to sail
anywhere in the world. I wondered how soon Melville
would be allowed to pin on the second epaulette showing
the world that he had been a post captain for three or more
years. If I were lucky, one of these days, I too could switch
the epaulette to the right shoulder. There was nothing else
I wished to tell the man. "Thank you, Captain Melville," I
said.

"You're welcome, Lieutenant St. John," he replied. "By
George, sir, those gun muzzles look quite large. I could almost swear that you have a battery of 24's trained down me
throat, but that's impossible, hah hah."

His condescending attitude was beginning to annoy me.
Call my ship a jackass brig, hah hah, indeed. "By Harry,
sir, you've got a good eye. Those are 24-pounders and
they're double shotted. Now that we know you're British,
I'll have the gun ports closed."

We parted company. When we left, he looked puzzled
as to how we could get a broadside of 24's into so frail a
ship. I was sure that the problem would cause him some
sleepless nights. As he disappeared over the horizon, I
began to feel guilty over my behavior. Damn it, I was acting just like young Hornswoggler.

We sailed into Portsmouth Harbor two days later. The
storm had blown us well off our course. Even so, it was a
slow passage, for the wind was from the wrong quarter and
we had to beat against it in a zigzag pattern, losing more
distance to the east and the return west than we made to

the north. I had planned on a grand entrance. It would have been a most impressive sight to see the little *Rapid* herding a prize almost four times as large. But we did not have the glory of escorting a fine prize with the English flag flying over the French. Instead, we were alone; I almost felt as if we were slinking into port, trying our best to be unnoticed; if the prize had been lost at sea, I would face a court-martial for losing most of my crew. As we sailed in, I looked around the familiar harbor. I suddenly felt elated. There, just off the starboard bow, I saw the *Little Dragon*. Hornswoggler had made it to port; the prize was safe; our prize money was safe; the other members of the crew were safe.

I wasn't the only one to see and recognize the ship. "Capting," shouted one man, "there's the ole *Draging*. Mr. 'Ornswoggler made it."

We pulled into a spot in the downs not too far from the prize and let fly the anchor cables. As twin water spouts splashed up, our signal flags started aloft and Mr. Morris began the salute to the admiral by firing blank charges. The signal requested the commander of the *Little Dragon* to report to the *Rapid*. I went below to change to my best uniform; I would be reporting to Admiral Akers ashore. By the time Mr. Hornswoggler was aboard the brig, I had dressed, shaved, and donned a wig. When I came up on the quarterdeck, he was there waiting for me. "Delighted to see you, Hornswoggler," I said. "Did you have any trouble with the storm?"

"No, sir. I was going to set out the anchors, but the bloody Frenchman had only one sheet anchor aboard and that was buried deep in the hold. One of our balls took the bower anchor from where she was catted on the bow. I couldn't anchor, so I just said, 'Put her before the wind, lads,' and we ran from the storm. We were lucky enough to outrun it."

Lucky—that was a choice bit of understatement. The prize crew was indeed fortunate to be alive. Ordering my gig made ready, I left Hornswoggler, saying, "I must report to the admiral." I was rowed ashore and made my way to his office. Admiral Akers was in, but he was busy. I had been seated for just a few minutes when Flags came out to speak with me. "Afternoon, Willoughby," I said.

"Good afternoon, St. John. Admiral Akers wanted me to tell you that he will be engaged for a while, but he wishes to see you. He would like you to wait; to make your stay less tedious, he has sent you several recent copies of the *Chronicle*."

I thanked the flag lieutenant and watched him leave. Picking up an issue of the *Chronicle*, I flipped it open to the vital statistics section. I wasn't interested in the obituaries; if I had been a post captain, I would have read them first to see who above me on the list had died. I would save them until after I had finished the list of promotions and assignments. The first name to catch my eye was William Gamble. Old "Holy Bill" had been promoted and was now a rear admiral. I next read the captain's section. Almost coincidental with Gamble's appointment, his cousin, Mr. Lloyd, had been posted as captain of a hulk used as a receiving ship. The old man had done well by Lloyd getting him to post rank at last. John Gamble had been posted too, and was now flag captain to his uncle aboard the *Royal George*, 98, a three-decker. I continued working my way through the list and when I reached the lieutenants' section, I confirmed what I had suspected. Mr. Perkins had passed his examination and was now the flag lieutenant to his uncle.

I continued to read the *Chronicle*, looking for other tidbits, but my mind was busy with the Gamble family. How happy I was no longer to be aboard the same ship, to have no contact with them. I was damned lucky to have survived my encounter with Captain Gamble. My ruminations were interrupted by Flags. He opened the inner door and said, "Lieutenant St. John, the admiral will see you now."

Akers seemed pleased to see me. He had done well from the cruise of the *Rapid*. He was especially pleased with our latest prize. "St. John, we shall purchase the *Little Dragon* into His Majesty's service. It is a fine ship and there will be much prize money, although we can't allow you head money on the French crewmen you released. Your decision to release them was proper. I wish we could give her to you, for it will be a post ship, but she has already been promised. I know that you shall be posted soon; I have suggested to the Admiralty that you be promoted, and I'm not without influence. You fought a gallant action against high odds and should be rewarded." He paused to clear his throat, then pulled a snuff box from his fob pocket. Taking a pinch of snuff on his finger, he inhaled it and sneezed loudly. "I'm afraid that I have some bad news for you; your independent cruise is over. I had hoped to give you another month, for you were doing well, but necessity dictates a change. I have new orders for you. You may open them once you are aboard your ship. I'll arrange to have your prize crew sent back to you and for you to indent for supplies. You will be sailing for Gibraltar in three days."

"Thank you, Admiral Akers."

"By the by, St. John, how do you put up with that scalawag midshipman of yours? I forget his name, but it is a most improbable one."

"Hornswoggler, sir?"

"Aye, that's his name and a most appropriate one it is. He pulled the most outrageous prank when he came ashore after anchoring the prize." The admiral started to laugh. "It seems, sir, that just before your man dropped anchor, a Dutch merchant ship foundered right here in the harbor.

When Hornswoggler came ashore, he noticed several of the Dutch seamen's bodies washed up on the bank. Telling his men to put the Dutchmen's hands into their pockets, he went into the Blue Anchor tavern and ordered a glass of wine. As he was drinking the wine, he spoke out, 'I always thought that Dutch seamen were a lazy lot. I found it to be true today. When their ship went down, the squareheads were too lazy to take their hands out of their pockets even to save their lives.' The captain of the Dutch ship was in the tavern too. He shouted at your midshipman, called him a liar, so Hornswoggler told him, 'If you don't believe me, just go out and see for yourselves.' A group of them left the tavern and sure enough, every one of those damned Dutchies had their hands in their pockets. The Dutch captain was so embarrassed that he left town."

I was more than a little disgusted with Hornswoggler. That was a sick prank, but from the admiral's reaction, many of the people here in Portsmouth thought it funny. If they had been English seamen instead of Dutch, Hornswoggler would have been in trouble. He had been successful in hornswoggling the Dutch captain, but to what purpose? One of these days, I hoped to stop his practical joking. It would have to be soon, if he were pulling pranks like this. I thanked the admiral again and left his office to return to my ship.

Once aboard the *Rapid*, I gave orders to have the revictualing done and told Horace Morris to make sure we still had enough powder and shot. Leaving the quarterdeck, I went to my cabin where I slit open the envelope and pulled out my orders; I stared at them incredulously. I was ordered to proceed to Gibraltar, as Admiral Akers had told me. When I got there, I was to report to the Honorable Rear Admiral Sir William Gamble, K.B.

Chapter 17

It was a balmy day in August. Oh, to spend the fall in England with the leaves turning red, then sere; what a pleasure that would be, but after autumn comes winter with its ice and snow. It was a beautiful dream, but I would not spend autumn and winter of 1795 at home; my orders were to sail today. By the time September and her squalls arrived in the Channel, I would be in the Mediterranean, the warm, sunny Mediterranean. My orders were such that I was free to "chase and capture any prizes encountered during my passage." I was to join the fleet under the command of Rear Admiral William Gamble. This distressed me, for Gamble would never recommend me for promotion. Unless Admiral Akers was able to persuade the Admiralty to act in my behalf, I would still be a lieutenant commanding at the conclusion of this war.

Younger men with political connections were being posted captain; some were as young as sixteen or seventeen. I was twenty-three years old and still a lieutenant; commander or not, I wasn't a post captain. Promotion wasn't for everyone; many men remained lieutenants until they died. I looked over the port rail; there to my east lay France. We were passing just outside of the Bay of Biscay where we had captured so many prizes just a few weeks back. I would rather have passed near Guernsey where I would have found an excuse to visit the widow Tallant. It was too late to do anything about Marie; I might as well make the best of the situation. "Mr. Hornswoggler," I said, "have the helmsman alter course three points to port. We will sail around the hoop of the bay."

"Aye aye, sir," said the young jackanapes.

It was almost noon, time for the sun to be shot, time for the watch to change. The ship's bell was struck eight times. A drove of seamen came rushing up from below, the slap, slap, slap of their horny, bare feet loud against the deck planking. With the men came Lieutenant Nicholas Pope. Pope had been assigned to the *Rapid* to replace poor Buckley. He was an older man, a much older and more phlegmatic man than I had expected. He had been commissioned lieutenant in 1779, but never had been posted. Pope seemed content to remain in his present station. He did not want the responsibilities of command. The man was twice as old as I, yet according to navy regulations, he was expected to take orders from me. What made it particularly awkward was the fact that we both were lieutenants despite the fact that I sported an epaulette on my left shoulder.

"Afternoon, Captain," said Pope as he came up on the quarterdeck. The man easily made three of Buckley; he was no taller, but his girth accounted for the difference. How he ever shoehorned his way into the tiny first lieutenant's cubicle was beyond me. Suffice it to say that he did. The man knew his seamanship, I must say. Set him to any task and he would perform it well, but to require any initiative of him would be asking too much. Pope would make an adequate replacement, but I missed the drive, the enthusiasm, even the uncertainties of a younger man.

There was no time to talk to Pope; the sun must be shot.

I checked it through my own sextant while Pope, Horn-swoggler, Dinsdale, and Smythe read the inclination too. Down on the deck, several of the seamen were using mariner's staffs to check the height of the sun. As soon as I looked over the midshipmen's results, I would announce the official reading to the crew. Everyone finished and put his instrument away. Smythe checked the midshipmen's calculations and gave me their readings. Not bad; both of the young gentlemen had calculated the latitude correctly. I announced the figure to the waiting seamen. Since we had no flaybottomist aboard the *Rapid*, the master had to take over the duties of teacher. As a pedant, Smythe was short-tempered. He set the midshipmen to work on a problem in trigonometry. It was something to do with the tangent to a line. I didn't hear him well enough to follow the entire problem, nor did I take time to check. Instead, I was pacing up and down the weather side of the quarterdeck, thinking about Old Gamble's reaction when I would report to him. I heard a loud noise coming from the lee; it was so vociferous a sound that it disrupted my thoughts. I swiveled around toward the noise. "You stupid young sod, you!" shouted Smythe to Hornswoggler.

It doesn't take much brain to be an outhouse cleaner, I thought, as I walked over to see what the problem was. Algebra and trigonometry were never Hornswoggler's long suit. He had messed up the problem completely. I watched as Smythe rather impatiently tried to explain where he had gone wrong. I wondered as I watched if Hornswoggler really knew how to do the problem and only made the mistake to exasperate Smythe. Knowing that the midshipman was a practical joker made me distrust him in every situation.

Before I could speak to Mr. Hornswoggler, the lookout hailed the deck. "Sail ho!" he shouted.

"Where away?" I shouted back.

"Four points off port bow, dead abeam."

I snatched a spyglass from its beckets and pulled it open with a loud snap. Pointing the extended, brass telescope over the rail, I adjusted the draw tube for focus. The ship sighted by the lookout was visible. It looked like an armed lugger and was headed directly for us. Luggers were frequently used by the French as privateers. They are large enough to hold many men, but easy to sail with few. I hadn't altered the rigging; the *Rapid* was still a brigantine. Since His Majesty seems to favor full-rigged ships for his naval service and no brigantines at all, to the best of my knowledge, the lugger probably thought we were a fat, foolish merchant ship. If I could keep him thinking that a bunch of jackasses were sailing the jackass brig until he came up, we could surprise and capture him. I estimated the distance between the two ships and calculated how far the *Rapid* would sail before we made contact with the other ship if we pretended to flee. It would be at least an hour, possibly two before we were within gun range.

"Beat to quarters," I shouted, "load all guns, but do not run out. Do not raise the port covers." The drummer started the beat on his drum; the rhythmic rattle pulsated throughout the ship, alerting every man. Partitions were knocked down, the decks sprinkled with sand, and water tubs pushed into place. The galley fire was doused over the far side of the ship where the lugger could not see what was done. Hoping to confuse the privateer longer, I took off my cocked hat and uniform coat. Standing there in my ruffled shirt, I found the weather warm enough for my costume. "Hoist the merchant recognition signal," I told young Dinsdale. The huge flags were run up; the wind, moderately fresh, blew the banners straight out from the masts where they could be clearly seen, but there was no answer from the lugger. "Make the Blue Peter ready, but run up the American flag now," I told the midshipman. The squeal of the halliards was loud in the silence as we ran up the American flag. America was neutral. Flying false colors didn't work; the lugger wasn't deterred; he continued to bore in toward us.

"Quarterdeck guns are loaded and ready, sir," said Mr. Hornswoggler.

"Port 'n starboard batteries 'r' loaded 'n ready, sir," called Mr. Pope from the gun deck.

"Do not fire until I give the signal for a lugger," I shouted back. The lugger was closer now. It was big, damned near as big as the *Rapid*, running at least one hundred twenty tons. The huge lugsails were well filled; it was a fast ship despite its stumpy look. A cannon aboard the enemy fired across our bow, hoping to force us to heave to. Judging by the sound, it was a 12-pounder. It was time to act. "Clew up the courses!" I shouted.

The topmen began to brail up the big, square, lower sails. Our speed started to drop, but we still had way. The lugger came up alongside; it was barely a pistol shot off. "Heave to, monsieur!" shouted a man whom I took to be the French captain. "Heave to, or we'll give you a broadside!"

"Hoist the Blue Peter," I told Mr. Midshipman Dinsdale. He started to pull on the halliard and the flag made its way up toward the masthead. Drawing my sword from its sheath, I shouted, "Raise gun hatches!" Nine hands yanked nine tricing ropes. The hatch covers rose smartly, loudly smacking against the hull of the brig as they were secured in place. Without further command, the gun crews of all nine carronades ran them out by pushing the slides forward. I missed the rumbling growl of wooden trucks on the oak deck, but then, the carronades were not long guns.

The elevation of the guns had been set for point-blank range; the enemy was only a pistol's shot away. "Fire!" I shouted.

My commands were repeated by Pope and Hornswoggler. The charges exploded when the hot sparks dropped from the flint to the priming quill and fire flashed into the heart of the powder charge. The charges exploded with a timber-shivering, thunderous roar. The guns had been double-shotted and each had a charge of nine grape atop the balls. Iron spheres are grape for a 24-pounder and weigh two pounds apiece. The grape and the large 24-pounder balls were hurled into the hull of the Frenchman, smashing through bulwarks to raise deadly clouds of splinters. Two guns aboard the lugger were overturned, one trapping part of its crew beneath its immense weight. Men were writhing on the lugger's deck as they screamed a threnody of pain. The devastation was fearful. They had not yet fired a gun, but even as my men were swabbing out the hot carronades with their sheepskin sponges and pushing fresh cartridges down the gaping maws, a weak broadside was fired "for the glory of the flag." Before we could answer, before the echo of the shots dimmed away, the Tricolor plunged to their deck. They had surrendered.

I sent Mr. Hornswoggler over to the lugger in the first cutter, while Mr. Pope checked our vessel for damage. The unwounded Frenchmen were docile and allowed themselves to be locked in the hold. The French captain, who was uninjured, was sent over to the *Rapid* together with the lugger's papers. As I had surmised, the craft was a French privateer. The war two and a half years old, it was difficult for an English privateer to make a living as most of the French merchant ships were rotting in ports. The coasting trade did offer some prizes, but it was still hard work. On the other hand, a French privateer had so many chances at rich merchant ships, he did not know which to chase first. While French commerce withered on the vine and turned into an internal affair, the commerce of England was booming. Hundreds of ships sailed under the English flag. Numerous French privateers sent the insurance rates into the atmosphere. Regardless of the cost of insurance, or the loss of many merchant ships, English merchants earned the money that would eventually win the war. As to the French privateers, their situation was very much like that of the old woman who went to the well too often. Sooner or later the Royal Navy caught up with them. Some might be wealthy after they were released from an English naval prison at the end of the war, or they might be unlucky and captured on their first cruise. I looked at the log; the lugger was the *Gauloise*. She carried seven guns, four swivels, and eighty-six men. Five of her crew had died in the broadside; eight were wounded.

We were not the first English ship to encounter the *Gauloise*. Their cruise had been successful prior to meeting us, judging from the English seamen locked in their hold as prisoners. When we had shoved the French sailors below, the English had come up to deck. The fifteen Englishmen we rescued would not cheer so loudly after I pressed them into the king's service. Their ship had been taken four days earlier; there was no hope of intercepting it and freeing their officers.

The sun blazed hot upon the two ships as repairs were made to the *Gauloise*. It wasn't much of a prize, having no rich cargo to increase the value of the ship, but I did discover the specie taken from several English prizes plus a small horde of golden "Looeys" that belonged to the French captain-owner. When that was added to the value of the ship and the head money, it was a respectable prize. I was feeling very content, almost smug, with myself. I had added to my crew and taken a prize too. When we joined the fleet at Gibraltar, I would be presenting Gamble with a nice sum of prize money. As the admiral under whose orders I sailed, he was entitled to one eighth of whatever the court awarded for the lugger. The ship was big enough to be bought into the king's service, but it should be armed more heavily. There was no use in trying to anticipate what it would bring. Let the seamen worry about how much prize money they would get. I had more important things to worry about.

Not wishing to risk the prize, I changed our course to weather La Coruña instead of completing the circuit of the bay. The weather continued nice as we sailed along the coast of Portugal. I would have liked to have stopped at Oporto to lay in a supply of the red nectar produced there, but decided that I had enough port wine without stopping. As we sailed, I drove the men to scrub the ship as it had never been cleaned before. We expended gallons of paint and turpentine. Topmen went aloft with buckets to tar the rigging. Decks were holystoned until they were white enough to reflect moonbeams like a mirror. I even had the main mast rerigged back to a brig for fear that the unorthodox rig of a hermaphrodite brig might raise Gamble's ire. Before we reached Gibraltar, the *Rapid* looked more like an artist's painting of a ship than a working, fighting brig of war.

At last we sailed into the roads at Gibraltar. It was a good entrance, the small brig herding a lugger as big as she. The captured lugger flew the English Blue Peter over the Tricolor to tell the world that it was a prize. We dropped anchor near several other British men-of-war. All of them were larger, much larger than the *Rapid*, but we looked smarter than any other ship in the anchorage. No sooner were we anchored than a flotilla of bumboats winged their

way toward us, bringing fresh fruit, illegal spirits, willing
women, and crews of the most dedicated thieves in Chris-
tendom. Gypsies have no more ability at stealing than the
boatmen who serve Gibraltar. Not having any marines on
the brig, I posted a seaman armed with a cutlass in front of
my door to protect the cabin and its contents. My personal
possessions taken care of, I made arrangements to protect
what ship's property I could by insisting that the crew and
passengers of only one bumboat be allowed on the ship at
any given time. The others would have to wait their turn.
With only a few of Gibraltar's fabled ladrones aboard, possibly we could keep an eye on them and prevent them from
making off with our property.

A large three-decker down the line from where we were
anchored flew the broad pennant of an admiral. I would
have to report my arrival. Before I could call for my gig, I
saw signal flags run up the liner's halliards. They were making our number. The flags changed as more were hoisted.
The captain of the *Rapid* was ordered to report aboard the
flagship. "Acknowledge," I said to the midshipman standing near me. "Acknowledge and then have my gig lowered."

The gig pulled toward the three-decker. The sun was
pleasant. It felt good to be alive, good to have completed
the first part of our voyage; but knowing that Admiral
Gamble was waiting for me aboard the liner made my
mood more funereal than the paint job of my gig. The
black oars bit the water in measured rhythm; we were near
the *Royal George* now. "Ahoy there!" shouted their lookout.

"*Rapid*," sang back Murphy. We hooked on and I
started scrambling up toward the covered entry port. It was
a second-rate ship of ninety-eight guns and towered three
decks above the orlop. To lower the center of gravity, the

builders had set each deck back, making the top gun deck narrower than the second, which was narrower than the third. This tumble home plus the additional height made it a laborious climb. At last, I reached the wooden steps cleated to the side of the ship. They started several feet below the port and had rope banisters. When I reached the step of the port, it was fenced and canopied. The portico cover was a bare five feet ten inches above the porch itself; I had to duck to enter. As I went through the entry there were no side boys wearing white gloves; there were no bosuns twittering away on their pipes. I was only a lowly commander; such honors were reserved for the elite who had been posted. There was a detachment of armed marines and Lieutenant Perkins waiting to greet me. Perkins looked no different than he had as a midshipman; only the uniform encasing his froglike body was changed. He wore a beatific smile that turned my guts to a block of ice. I stood there looking at him; he looked back, his tongue flitting in and out between his lips, which were curved into a nasty smirk. "Lieutenant St. John," he said, "I am delighted to inform you that you are under arrest."

Chapter 18

To say that I was surprised by being arrested would have been a gross understatement; I was stunned, flabbergasted, astonished, astounded, amazed, dumbfounded, and confounded, but more than anything else, I was frightened. I had only arrived on station; I could think of no grounds for Admiral Gamble's action other than his strong dislike of me. Although no one told me what the charge was, or who had made it, I was firmly convinced that "Holy Bill" was at the root of my trouble. "What charges?" I had asked Perkins, but received no answer.

Perkins relieved me of my sword and had the marines take me below to a small cubicle. Some unfortunate lieutenant had been dispossessed to make room for me. I sat on his cot and pondered my problem. With no charge explained to me, how could I defend myself? All I knew was that very soon the court-martial flag would be flying. A panel of judges composed of all the captains and admirals on station would be gathered around a long table in the great cabin of the *Royal George*. My crimes, whatever they were, would be read to the court and I hoped I would have a chance to reply. I hoped, I said, for not always was the accused given the right to a defense. Such an oversight would be grounds for reversal, but even if a guilty verdict were reversed, the stigma of a court-martial would cling to me closer than even my own skin. I might wind up disgraced and on the beach for the remaining years of my life. I was not being unduly pessimistic. An acquaintance of mine, Captain Matthew Smith of the *Diomede*, was so accused. He was cleared at a later date, but even now Captain Smith is unemployed by the service and has been so for the past few years. I wonder if he will ever wipe out the stigmata caused by false, vicious claims against his honor.

Time passes slowly when there is nothing to do. I wished for a book to read or a fellow human with whom I could make conversation. Reaching into my fob pocket, I pulled out my watch. The time was 10:37 A.M. I closed the cover and returned the watch to the pocket; I started to pace, but the cabin was too small for effective pacing, so I dropped myself back on the cot. At last I tried to exercise my memory by reciting poetry. I had always liked Beaumont and Fletcher's *Hoisting the Sails*.

> *Lay her before the wind, up with your canvas,*
> *And let her work, the wind begins to whistle;*
> *Clap all her streamers on, and let her dance*
> *As if she were the minion of the ocean.*
> *Let her bestride the billows, till they roar,*
> *And curl their wanton heads.*
> *The day grows fair and clear, and the wind*
> *   courts us.*
> *O! for a lusty sail now, to give chase to,*
> *A stubborn bark, that would but bear up to us,*
> *And 'change a broadside bravely!*

Heady stuff that, solid realistic, the type of poem I appreciated. I could smell the salt air, feel the ship working beneath my feet as the wind blew fresh in the rigging. The lookout's hail, the chase, the exchange of broadsides between the ships, it was real, as real as if the poet had lived it. I cast about for another to recite, but my memory failed. No, trying to remember poetry was not the way to pass time more quickly. It was just as well that I stopped declaiming verse out loud, for there was a knocking at the door. "Enter," I called.

The door of the cabin opened and in came Lieutenant John Gamble, now Captain Gamble. He was as big as ever, too big for the tiny cubicle, but now that he wore the epaulette of a captain, he no longer had the sloppy, relaxed look I remembered. Behind him came Pierce Hallowell, who looked even gaunter than the last time I had seen him. Of course, he may just have looked more emaciated standing in the shadow of Gamble. "St. John," said the captain, "I see that my uncle has finally got you."

"Aye, sir, that he has. Congratulations on your promotion."

"Congratulations will be due me, St. John, when I get my own ship with my uncle no longer near me. Until then, the only change has been in the uniform."

"I wouldn't say that, sir. At least you no longer have Mr. Lloyd to contend with."

"You're right, St. John. The Lord has been merciful in that respect. Enough about me, what kin I do for you?"

"I have not been informed of the charges. How can I defend myself, sir, without knowing what to defend?"

"My uncle, the admiral, is charging you with stealing a chronometer when you left the *Monmouth*."

"Stealing? That's ridiculous. My chronometer was a gift from my uncle, Vice Admiral Bacon, when first I joined the Navy. I had it all the while I was with Pellew, but he is not here to testify for me. It does have a presentation engraving on the inside back cover."

"St. John, I would like to be your 'friend at court,' but I

cannot, for I will be solicitor for the Admiralty. I brought young Hallowell with me; he will be your 'friend.'"

With a friend as hesitant as Hallowell, I didn't need an enemy. Old "Holy Bill" could just leave my defense to that young nincompoop and not worry about the charges. I needed a Charles Fox, a William Pitt—either the younger or the elder—to plead my case and I was being offered a tongue-tied lieutenant. My doubts must have shown in my face, for Gamble spoke again. "As solicitor, I introduce the evidence. Even if I didn't like you, St. John, I would present both sides just to frustrate my uncle."

He was right. He had always been a friend, a good friend; I would have to trust him. "Whatever you say, sir. I don't know what to do. There is not time to send to London for the records from Mr. Arnold's shop."

"Have no fear, St. John. I know who was behind this plot and how to expose him. You will be exonerated."

That was easy for him to say, but I still had to face the court-martial. Having the solicitor for the Admiralty on my side would help, but damn it, he wasn't one of the judges. Hallowell and Gamble left; I went back to my musing.

The trial was held the next day. I woke to find Murphy in my cabin. He had brought my best uniform with him. The cox'n must have stayed up half the night heating a flat iron in the galley and pressing the uniform after sponging it. Dressed, I looked as fresh and crisp as a proper flag lieutenant. My hip felt naked without the sword, but until the court-martial was over, I would have to do without. I had breakfasted in the cabin on a tray; there was nothing else to do until I was called.

Lieutenant Perkins escorted me with a detachment of marines to the great cabin. He was treating me as if I were a common criminal. I would have given my parole, if asked, but he preferred to humiliate me. I would have been happy to return the favor if circumstances permitted.

As I entered the great cabin, I saw my sword lying lengthwise on the long table behind which sat my judges in awesome splendor. Each shoulder was covered with gold braid, for all of these men were senior captains. I saw no admiral behind the table, then realized that Admiral Gamble would be a witness for the prosecution. Better that than have him judge me. I looked at the men who would be judging me. There was Captain Forester of the *Saracen* sitting in the center of the table; he was the president of the court. Forester had the sour look of the congenital dyspeptic. He would rather spend a sovereign than a smile; his reputation was that of a man close with every farthing. I took one look at him and saw myself convicted, disgraced, and discharged from the service.

The charges against me were read out to the court. I was then allowed to take my seat at a small table next to Lieutenant Hallowell. I was frightened, really frightened; my stomach was tied in a tight sheepshank knot. I think that spending an hour on the quarterdeck in the middle of a battle would have been preferable to half an hour in court.

Mr. John Gamble, then, as solicitor for the admiralty began the proceedings by calling on the first witness, Admiral, Sir William Gamble, K.B.

Q. Admiral, in February of this year of our Lord, 1795, were you then captain of the *Monmouth*, 64?

A. I was, and did hold that situation at the date mentioned.

Q. Was Mr. St. John aboard your ship at this time, sir, and if so, in what capacity?

A. Yes, he was, as fourth lieutenant.

Q. When did you first miss the chronometer, sir?

A. The day after Mr. St. John left the ship.

Q. Did you miss the instrument yourself, or was its absence drawn to your attention?

A. The loss of the chronometer was reported to me by Acting Lieutenant Perkins.

Q. Admiral, do you have a receipt or bill of sale for the instrument?

The admiral grew very angry and started to splutter. "Mr. Gamble, sir, you insult me. Is not my word sufficient?"

"Sir, said Solicitor Gamble, "your word is good, but to establish all the facts, I have to ask you questions."

A. Very well, I do not have the bill of sale here. It is probably in my house at London.

Q. Will you please tell the court when and where you acquired the chronometer in question.

A. I purchased it in London from Mr. John Arnold. It was near the end of the American War. That would be 1783, I believe.

Q. If you did not have the bill of sale here, how did you happen to have the serial number?

A. I had an inventory taken in March, this year. I have the serial numbers of all three of my chronometers, my sextant, my pocket watch, and even my boarding pistols, written on that inventory.

Q. Who took the inventory?

A. Lieutenant Perkins, at that time Midshipman Perkins.

Q. Was the instrument engraved?

A. No, I would not waste money on engraving.

At this point, the solicitor stopped asking questions and asked if either I or my "friend at court" wished to cross-examine before he continued. We did not. All the questions we could have asked had already been asked.

The solicitor pulled several sheets of paper from an envelope, and speaking to Captain Forester, he said, "Mr. President, I wish to introduce these documents into evidence before I continue questioning the witness."

"What are these documents?" asked Forester.

"A survey that I conducted among the board members here. It shows the type of chronometer owned by each of you, the make, and where purchased, the year of purchase, and the serial number of the instrument."

I couldn't see why it would make any difference to my defense if Captain Forester of the *Saracen* or Captain Roberts of the *Phoebe* or even Captain Kent of the *Ardent* owned a chronometer, much less what use the serial number or date of purchase would do to help me. While Gamble, the solicitor, was speaking, I looked at the captains who made up the court. Captain Roberts I had never met before. He was a handsome man with a long slender nose and well-formed lips; he looked as elegant as Mr. Lloyd had aboard the *Monmouth*. I hoped that this man judging me had more brains than old Lloyd. The only judge I had met before was a Captain Dana. I knew him mainly by reputation; we had only exchanged half a dozen words at a reception. He was known through the fleet as the harshest captain afloat. He flogged more men in a day than all the other captains behind the table did in a week. From a man like this, I could expect little mercy. My only hope was that he didn't look like a Methodist; his nose was very red and filled with broken veins. I knew that "Holy Bill" was not too well liked among the captains and admirals of the fleet. Most of them thought that religion was very well in its place and its place was of a Sunday. I'm not trying to imply that the naval service was anti-religion, but to state that there were few fanatics like Gamble afloat and that those few were well disliked by the rest of the Navy.

Captain Forester accepted the documents. I thought that there were several pages, but as Gamble passed out one page to each judge, I realized that a separate copy had been made for each. All of the judges looked at the paper. Some seemed to study it carefully, while others just gave it a cursory look. Then the questioning started again.

Q. Admiral Gamble, the instrument missing, the one you purchased in 1783, bears the serial number 2415, is that correct, sir?

A. Yes, according to my inventory, that is the correct number.

Q. How are you sure that the instrument in question is the one you purchased in 1783?

A. On the inventory, the missing chronometer is marked as the spare. I used the other two, the newer ones, and kept the oldest instrument in reserve. I didn't even know that it was missing until I was informed by Mr. Perkins.

Q. When the loss was reported, you immediately thought that Lieutenant St. John was responsible?

A. We found the instrument in his possession, did we not?

"We did find an instrument in his possession, Admiral, but as you have not yet identified that instrument as yours other than reading the serial number from your inventory, I would like you to look at it." Mr. Solicitor Gamble handed the chronometer to his uncle. "Look at it, sir; look at it carefully. Is this your missing instrument?"

Admiral Gamble studied the watch closely. He opened the front cover and then the back cover. "Sir," he said, "the serial number is the same as that on my inventory, but this is not my chronometer. My instrument had a deep scratch on the back cover and did not have a presentation engraving on the inside of that cover. According to the inscription, this was given to St. John in 1793 by his uncle, Vice Admiral Bacon."

The president of the court, Captain Forester, said, "I move that we dismiss the charges."

"Mr. President," said the Admiralty's solicitor, "I would prefer to read the rest of the evidence including testimony from Mr. Perkins, who took the inventory, into the record. I would not like Lieutenant St. John to leave with a besmirched record."

"Proceed," said Forester.

"The exhibit presented to the court shows when several of the members of the court purchased Arnold chronometers. The list is arranged in chronological order by the date of purchase. If you will look at the list, you will see that the serial numbers progress chronologically too. If we fit the serial number of the instrument engraved with Mr. St. John's name into this list, we see that it would have had to be purchased in the period of 1792–94, which agrees with the inscription. Admiral Gamble's missing instrument was purchased back during the American War; it would have had a low serial number, no greater than number 200, I would venture, based on the purchase date of 1783 and the serial number of 314 for Captain Forester's instrument, which he acquired in 1788."

"Your statement makes sense, Mr. Gamble," said Captain Forester. "It is noted that it would have been impossible for this instrument in question to have been purchased in 1783. Therefore the court must conclude that the number on the inventory is a mistake. Whether the error was intentional or not, we do not know, but after questioning the man who took the inventory and reported the instrument missing, we may know more. Is Mr. Perkins available?"

"He is flag lieutenant to Admiral Gamble," said Captain Gamble.

"Pass the word for Mr. Perkins," said Forester.

I sat back in my chair, waiting to see Perkins put on the spot, but there was a whispered conference between the judges. I was sent from the room as Perkins entered. I was disappointed; I did so want to see his reaction when questioned, but I was taken to the quarterdeck of the *Royal George* by Hallowell. "You're cleared," he said, "but we have to wait for the formal verdict. Since you are technically still a prisoner, give me your parole and you may remain above decks. I'm going back to the great cabin to listen to the conclusion of the trial."

"My parole is gladly given, Mr. Hallowell, on the condition you tell me what transpired when you next have a chance."

I knew that I was exonerated, but my stomach didn't. It was still churning. Perkins remained in the great cabin for a full half hour. I was in a good position to watch the door from where I paced. When he made his exit, he looked but one stage removed from death. I had always disliked the clot, but he was so shaken that I almost felt sorry for him. He sneered at me as he passed in sight of the quarterdeck and then made a rude, seaman's gesture with his finger that canceled any sympathy I had felt for him. I learned all of the details much later. Young Perkins had almost been attacked by his uncle the admiral. "Holy Bill" was incensed because he realized that his younger nephew was, "bearing false witness." That made it a crime against God as well as against that sinner, St. John. The old admiral had his faults, but other than putting me and other sinners into a dangerous situation, he wasn't too bad. We were in the

business of fighting the enemy. I couldn't even hold shoving me to the forefront of battle against the man. When
he found what his nephew had done to me, he apologized.
Not to be outdone, I apologized right back to him. While
I never would be Gamble's favorite officer, we did come to
an understanding.

Shortly after Perkins left the deck, I was called back to
the great cabin. Although I knew that I had been cleared,
my eyes immediately went to my sword, which had lain on
the table all through the trial. Would it be hilt or point
facing me? The haft was pointed toward me as I entered; I
was exonerated. I could feel the muscles of my stomach
loosen up from the violent spasm that had accompanied
my pacing of the deck. I was adjudged innocent. In fact,
the court went so far as to say that I have been accused
by error. They should have charged Perkins with mal-
feasance, but he was the admiral's nephew. I dropped all
charges, allowing him to resign his commission without
having to face a trial. I could have insisted on charging
him, but I would rather forget Mr. Perkins than renew the
active enmity of "Holy Bill." I still wasn't his favorite
lieutenant by a long way. In fact, I think he resented me
even more after the trial than he did before.

I was glad to leave the *Royal George.* Murphy had my
gig waiting and seemed excited to see me. As we headed
toward the *Rapid,* I wondered what new trouble Admiral
Gamble planned for me.

Chapter 19

Time since the trial hung heavy on my hands. I had been exonerated, but now I seemed to be thrust into some kind of limbo. Why the admiral was waiting, I didn't know, but it was bad to have my men penned aboard ship, unable to sample the delights of the Rock. The *Rapid* was the least significant of Gamble's fleet. With luck, he might send us somewhere to deliver dispatches. Until then, the port of Gibraltar was a sultry hell fed by the furnaces of Africa. Even wind scoops did little to cool the ship.

As I thought about the muggy heat, I saw a burst of color erupt at the masthead of the *Royal George*. All captains were summoned to the flagship for a conference. I called for my gig. Once aboard the three-decker, we were given orders to sortie in the Mediterranean. No one told me if the French were out or if we were just showing the flag. I returned to my ship and ordered her out to sea.

The fleet passed into the Mediterranean; I could see the Spanish coastline off our portside. They had been our allies, but now were under the dominion of France. We had not gone too far past Algeciras when the wind freshened to a gale. The storm was totally unexpected. I was glad that we had not rerigged the *Rapid* to a brig. As a brigantine, we did not have to send down the topmasts as they were not up. The force of the wind was increasing logarithmically; I knew that we were in for a real blow. The master, Mr. Smythe, appeared on the quarterdeck. "Capt'n," he shouted over the noise of the wind, "this un's goin' t' be a real blow."

I nodded at Smythe. I had reached that conclusion myself. The master considered himself a weather witch, but he had not predicted the storm. He was busy telling everyone how bad it would be to save some credit for his weather knowledge. It was a harmless conceit. I said nothing to him about it. I looked around the sea; where just an hour before we had ships in sight in all directions, now the *Rapid* was alone. I ordered more canvas taken in. We were battened down and had plenty of sea room. We would try to ride out the fury.

Fury it was, ever increasing. As the winds blew, they brought rain, rain by the hogshead, rain by the tun. The waves grew in size, grew drastically, lifting the sloop up and dropping it down, tossing it high into the air and letting it fall with a timber-shivering crunch into the trough. It wasn't only an up and down motion, but a gyrating, twisting movement that threatened to shake the masts out of the vessel. Thank the Lord we had our canvas in early for it would be a crime to send men up in this maelstrom. We bobbed and tossed for two nights and a day while lightning flared and an upending stream of water, like a mighty waterfall, fell upon us; bedding was sodden, clothing soaked, and the men miserable, but there was no relief in sight. I was beginning to feel like Noah, but he had forty such days and nights.

At last the rain stopped, but the sea was covered by a light fog. I ordered a roll taken; we had lost no one, though we came close when a waister was washed off the ship by one wave and neatly deposited back on deck by the next.

Like Gamble had done when we faced a storm in the *Monmouth*, I had put the ship before the wind. Had I not done so, I'm sure that we would have turned turtle after being swamped by some of the waves. The storm over, we began to restore the ship to a state of battle readiness. The fleet had been sailing for Leghorn. Undoubtedly, the other ships would rendezvous there. I gave orders to sail for the boot of Italy. The *Rapid* heeled over on the new tack. We were making good time. Murphy came up on the quarterdeck bringing me a biscuit and a cup of hot tea. As he handed them to me, I saw a strange expression on his face. I was about to say something to him when he said, "Hssst, sair, is that guns I be hearing?"

I strained my ears; yes it was the sound of guns, I could hear them clearly. "Helmsman," I said, "steer for the sound of the guns."

The *Rapid* heeled over on the port tack. Yards were hauled 'round to catch the wind. The change in course put the wind on the other side of the brigantine. What had been the weatherside of the quarterdeck was now the lee; I crossed over to the new weather side while the other officers crossed to the new lee. Extra lookouts were sent aloft. If we were sailing to the guns, we were sailing into possible action. "Mr. Hornswoggler," I called, "beat to quarters."

As we continued to sail, the sound of the cannon grew louder and more frequent, as if a stern chase had been concluded and they were now fighting broadside to broadside. There was still a mild mist over the sea limiting visibility to a little less than two cable lengths from where I stood. "Deck ahoy!" shouted the lookout, "I sees 'em nar, not three cables off. Ut's the *Monmouth*, sir; she's fightin' a French 74. They's another ship too, a three-decker, but she's been dismasted."

The sloop's motion carried us along rapidly, cutting through the fine mist. I could now see the outlines of the two ships; they were fighting broadside to broadside. The guns of the *Monmouth* seemed to be firing faster than the guns of the Frenchman, but how could a comparatively frail 64-gun ship stand up to the might of a 74? The French ship not only had more guns, but those on his lower gun deck were much larger than the 24-pounders of the *Monmouth*. As I looked at the ships, I recognized the dismasted vessel; it was the *Royal George*, Admiral Gamble's flagship. I also saw a broad blue pennant flying from fo'top of the *Monmouth*. It was easy to see what had happened. The *George* had shaken her masts out during the storm. The *Monmouth* had found her and was towing her to a dockyard, probably Gibraltar. Admiral Gamble had transferred his flag to the 64-gun ship.

I turned my telescope to the *George*; there was a string of small boats out, trying to tow the three-decker into position to join the battle. I was sure that I could recognize the form of Captain John Gamble in the foremost of the boats. If the French could be stalled for a short time, the *George* could be towed up and the battle would end with the Frenchman retreating. It didn't look like John Gamble could get the ponderous hulk into position in time. I had an idea, but it was foolhardy; no, it was even worse, it was suicidal. If I brought the *Rapid* into action, I could purchase the time necessary for the *George* to come into position, but the cost would be severe.

For some reason, I started to think of the French privateers who had the audacity to attack my ship from fishing boats. It would be as big a gamble for me to pit the *Rapid* against a 74 as it had been for them to attack me. I could sail from the fight and no one would ever criticize me for doing so. Brigs of war are not expected to

tackle ships of line. Still, thinking about the fishing boats
reminded me that we had not been able to bring our
guns to bear on them. That was the answer. "Mr. Hornswoggler, you will load the quarterdeck carronades with
canister. Two bags of musket balls per gun should do the
trick." I turned from him and hollered down at the main
deck, "Mr. Pope, please load the broadside guns with
double shot!"

"Aye aye, sir," called back Pope.

The battle was too hot and heavy for either ship to
notice as I conned the *Rapid* in athwart the stern of the
Frenchman. Heavy clouds of acrid smoke hung over both
ships. I could hear the sounds of men working the guns,
the explosion of charges, and voices. We were close enough
to the thick glass of the stern windows for me to extend
my arm over the rail and touch the gallery rail. "Heave-to!"
I shouted. The waisters pulled the yards 'round and we
were ready to open fire. The 74 towered far up above us
like a cliff of granite, the rail even with our mast top. "Mr.
Pope, open fire when ready. Aim high through the stern
window. Mr. Hornswoggler, hold your fire until I call
for it."

"Fire!" shouted Pope. Seven 24-pounder carronades, all
double-shotted, exploded, sending fourteen heavy balls
through the glass window, smashing the glass into thou-
sands of flying shards. The guns were angled upward; the
balls pierced the decks, coming out on the quarterdeck.
One of them must have struck the man at the helm, for
the French ship started to swing out of control, but seconds
later it was righted. By this time, Pope had fired a second
broadside, raking the gun deck of the 74. I could hear their
volume of fire slacken and the keening screams of the
wounded. We must have overturned some of their guns.
Someone aboard the French ship ran to the stern guns to

fire at the mosquito that was bothering them, but the guns couldn't be depressed enough to hit us. Both of them went off, the balls passing well overhead. I heard someone call for boarders; they started to assemble at the stern rail of the French liner. Standing as we were, almost touching the stern of the enemy, the boarders could drop down or climb down our mast onto the *Rapid*. The French boarding party was formed and ready to come over the rail; Mr. Nutley and some of his bosun's mates pushed against the stern of the Frenchman with barge poles. The gap between the ships widened even as the first of the boarders was leaping. He missed the mast and fell into the widening gap, plunging down into the water like an anchor. The other boarders were dazed by our maneuver. The distance between the ships was much wider now.

"Mr. Hornswoggler," I shouted, "now, if you please." He fired both of the quarterdeck carronades. The musket balls cut through the boarding party as a scythe cuts through ripe grain. Those who could move were driven back, the others lay in limp piles on the deck. Now that we were away from the other ship, they could depress their stern guns to fire at us, but our helmsman kicked the rudder down and we closed the gap until we were almost snubbed up alongside them. The stern guns went off harmlessly. The Frenchman called for boarders again. Once more we pushed the two ships apart, but it was not necessary to fire; the boarding party turned tail and ran for safety as soon as they realized that we could fire at them again.

While we were playing ducks and drakes with the boarding party, Pope kept up the raking of the 74, alternating between angling balls at the enemy's quarterdeck and raking the gun decks. He had fired six such broadsides and was ready for the seventh. As Pope gave his gun crews the

BEFORE THE WIND 187

order to fire, young Mr. Dinsdale called me to the side of
the boat. Seeing what I was doing, John Gamble had
abandoned towing the *Royal George*. His boats were now
lying alongside the *Rapid*. I knew that with Gamble's two
hundred men we were in a position to board.

He came up to the quarterdeck, large as ever. "Mr.
Hornswoggler, you may fire your canister down the gun
deck," I said. "John, are you ready to board?"

"Aye, St. John," he answered.

While we fired yet another broadside, the men made
ready. It was over the rail of the *Rapid*, through what had
been the stern window of the Frenchman. Screaming their
hearts out the Rapids and the Georges dashed into the
French ship. The sudden presence of well over two hundred fifty boarders carried those Frenchmen on the deck
before them like a high tidal wave carries flotsam. I was
howling as loud as any Jack Nasty Face as I started up the
ladder to reach the main deck. A Frenchman interposed
himself between me and the deck, aiming a pistol directly
at me. Before he could fire, I thrust out my sword and
skewered him. At last, I was up on the main deck with the
others right behind me.

Boarding was a foolhardy trick. We stood the chance
of being fired on by the *Monmouth*. Possibly our yelling
told them what was happening, because they stopped firing
and started to board the French ship to help us. The
French were completely demoralized. Some fought bravely;
others threw down their weapons. Captain John Gamble
himself cut the French flag down. When the Tricolor fell,
all resistance ceased. We were in control of the French
ship.

I looked around the 74; it was a shambles. Between the
Rapid's guns and those of the *Monmouth*, we had over-

turned almost half the big ship's guns. Dead and dying
French seamen were heaped around the deck. I knew that
my vessel had taken little damage, shielded as we were
from the liner's fire, but I wondered how badly hurt the
Monmouth was.

The surviving Frenchmen were soon all locked below, except for the wounded. Our surgeon and the French surgeon were doing their best for these unfortunates. John
Gamble had sent a boat back to the hulk of the *George*
to fetch his surgeon over to help, but directed him to the
Monmouth first to see if he were needed there. As the
decks were cleared of the dead, the ship began to take on
a semblance of normalcy. There was extensive damage to
the French ship, the *Ville de Marseille*, but mostly in the
hull where all of the *Rapid*'s balls and most of the *Monmouth*'s had struck. With the extra manpower available
from the crew of the *George*, repairs were going briskly.
At John Gamble's urging, I went with him aboard the
Monmouth to see how she had fared. The 64 had sustained
the brunt of the casualties, having sixty-seven killed and one
hundred ten men wounded. My butcher's bill was much
lower; I had lost only three killed and six wounded during
the boarding while the Georges lost eight killed and fourteen wounded in the same action. The heaviest casualties
fell to the Frenchman, who lost well over two hundred
killed and close to three hundred wounded. He had been
caught in a cross fire; it would have been more prudent
for him to have surrendered earlier, but both the first and
second captains had been killed; the lieutenant who took
over was prevented from striking by a political officer.

The *Ville de Marseille* was not the only ship to lose
officers. Aboard the *Monmouth*, the captain fell in the
first broadside. All four lieutenants were either killed or
wounded. When I heard this, I worried about Mr. Hal-

lowell for a second, then remembered that he was serving on the *George*. With all the officers out of action, Admiral Gamble had taken command of the ship and with the aid of a brace of midshipmen continued the fight against the 74. For a psalm-singing, overly pious, elderly gentleman, it was a feat akin to that of Samson swinging the jawbone of an ass to destroy his enemies. I had always marked Gamble as overly cautious, as a political captain, but now I knew that I had misjudged him.

The *Monmouth* was in bad shape, as bad as the *Ville de Marseille*, at first glance. John Gamble ordered the boats back to the *George* to bring back more seamen to help with the repairs. As we looked around the ship, we saw that our first impression was incorrect. The French ship had fired high, on the uproll, damaging the rigging severely, but other than on the deck and the quarterdeck there was little hull damage. We did not find the admiral at first, but shortly after we arrived, he came out of the captain's cabin. "Good day, John, and you too, St. John. Now that the battle is over, I have been thanking God for our deliverance."

Repairs to the *Monmouth* and the *Ville de Marseille* were completed in three hours. Both were ready to sail. To handle the four ships back to Gibraltar would involve a shifting of men. John Gamble proposed letting the French 74 tow the hulk of the *George*. He would move most of the *George*'s crew to the *Ville*. If we ran into any other French men-of-war, we would have a functioning 74 to fight them. He also proposed that the *Monmouth* tow the *Rapid*. By adding my crew to those of the 64-gun ship that were still able, we would have enough to man her too. Only two midshipmen were available of the *Monmouth*'s officers; I would be the acting captain. The admiral would once again shift his flag, this time to the prize which would be captained by his nephew, Captain Gamble. The plan suited me, but it would seem strange to be acting captain of the ship that held so many unpleasant memories.

"If your plan meets the approval of the admiral, John," I told him, "I'm more than willing."

The two of us went in search of "Holy Bill." We looked all over but did not find him until one of the seamen said, "I things 'e's below decks sir, down in the cockpit."

The fight was over; repairs were in the capable hands of Captain John Gamble. Old "Holy Bill," Bible in hand, was visiting the wounded, trying to give comfort to those who would not recover. "Uncle," said John Gamble, "may we talk with you?"

"Aye, Nephew," said the older man. "I'm almost done here. I'll meet you and Mr. St. John on the quarterdeck in ten minutes."

It was a long ten minutes; it probably was closer to twenty. At the last the admiral appeared; he was mining his nose as he walked toward us. "Gentlemen," he said.

John Gamble explained his plan, saying, "That will give us two capital ships to defend with if we meet any more of the French."

"Approved, John," said the admiral. "And you, sir, Mr. St. John, you could have gone off and left us to be taken by the French. No one expects a cockleshell like your brig to take on a 74. That was a most foolhardy thing for you to do, sir, but I am deeply grateful. I would have hated to have been thrown into a French prison, especially since we capture so few French admirals to exchange."

"It was a calculated risk, sir. As long as the *Monmouth* kept the Frenchman busy, he had little time for me."

"It was still beyond the call of duty, St. John. I shall mention you and your conduct most favorably in my dispatches; I shall also urge that you be posted as soon as possible. Now, St. John, that's as close as you'll get to the apology I owe you. It would be most unseemly for an admiral to apologize to a commander."

For Gamble, that was a handsome apology; I could expect no more. "Thank you, sir," I said.

The admiral smiled back at me; he looked as if he were about to laugh. "By the bye, St. John," he said, "you will hold a special thanksgiving church service aboard the *Monmouth* as soon as you are under way."

Maybe the old bird was right? I did have much to be thankful for. At least he had not told me to conduct daily services. "Aye aye, sir," I told him, for an admiral is always right whether one agrees with him or not.

We were soon on our way to Gibraltar. I was most exuberant as I paced the quarterdeck of the old *Monmouth*. Admiral Gamble was no longer my enemy. Soon I should be posted. Yes, I had good reason to be thankful.

Epilog

Two months after we delivered the prize, the hulk, and our two ships to Gibraltar, we received word from the Admiralty. The admiral had been using the *Ville de Marseille* as his flagship, for it was larger than any of the other 74's available to him. The prize had been purchased into His Majesty's service. The *Royal George* had been given a makeshift repair job and had sailed back to England for a complete rebuilding. I had continued as acting captain of the *Monmouth*. Soon, I would be either replaced or confirmed in that position. I wished for a sleek, fast frigate rather than the ungainly two-decker, but of necessity would take whatever the Admiralty offered, even demotion back to the *Rapid*.

The orders came at last from London along with a two-epaulette captain to take over the *Monmouth*. I was disappointed at first, for I thought that I had been forgotten. After the new man read himself in, he handed me a canvas envelope. I had been posted; the date of my new rank was the day I had taken command of the *Monmouth*, the day we captured the French 74. I was to proceed back to England, to Portsmouth, where I would take command of His Majesty's frigate *Cerberus*, 28. I was elated and allowed myself to daydream. With a fast frigate, even a 28-gun, 12-pounder frigate, I would be willing to sail anywhere. If the Admiralty ordered me to do so, I would gladly sail the *Cerberus* up the River Styx to the very gates of Hades, confident that I would be able to sail her back home with Charon's barge my prize.